Montana Delta Rodeo Cowboy: Bodyguard Protector

Debra Parmley

Montana Delta Rodeo Cowboy: Bodyguard Protector

Debra Parmley

Cover artist: Sheri L. McGathy

Formatted using Velum's Zephyr, for the western winds of Montana and Wyoming.

Published by Belo Dia Publishing Inc.

First edition. July 4, 2025

This book is dedicated to my friend and beta reader,
Charlene Leber Lancaster,
with gratitude and appreciation for her support, help, and
advice.
This book would not have been finished and published in
time without her help.

Chapter One

"I'm sending you out west, to Montana."

Emma Smith's boss Clement Oakley Esquire spoke from behind her, startling Emma from the letter she was typing, and she jumped.

She hadn't heard him leave his office.

"What?" Emma shook her head, thinking she hadn't heard him right. "You're sending me somewhere?"

He'd never done that before, or even talked about sending her somewhere.

"Yes, to Montana."

Her jaw dropped. She'd heard right. He was sending her to Montana. "Why?"

The lawyer presented the airline ticket with a flourish and placed it on her desk.

"I decided you deserved a getaway."

He corrected himself. "A holiday."

He smiled. "You've been a great secretary."

Getaway? What?

Then she realized he'd spoken in the past tense.

Been a great secretary? What does he mean, been? Oh no.

She needed this job.

"Are you, f-firing me?"

She barely got the words out as her cheeks heated with embarrassment.

She'd never been fired before.

What would she tell her family? Her friends?

Rent on her apartment had just gone up, she had her car payment, insurance, and credit card bills.

She couldn't be getting fired now.

What will I do?

Her thumb reached for the place on her other thumb where her nail polish had started to chip away and dug at it.

A nervous habit she sometimes wasn't aware she was doing.

"No. Of course not." He shook his head. "Don't be silly."

She paused her thumb from the destructive progress.

"Happy Birthday!" The joviality in his voice sounded forced. "You do have a birthday coming up."

"Oh!" Her eyebrows rose in surprise.

I wasn't aware he knew when my birthday was. He's never mentioned it before.

She'd worked for him for three years, and this seemed out of character for him.

But she didn't want to appear ungrateful.

What a generous gift. Much more than the typical card and fresh flowers.

How odd though.

After never acknowledging her birthday even once, now suddenly he was giving her this gift.

"Well, thank you," she said, amazed.

She glanced at the ticket.

The flight to Bozeman, Montana left early Monday morning. Today was Friday.

Just two full days to get ready. Why such short notice? What if I'd had other plans for my birthday?

He hadn't asked if she was free to go. Or wanted to.

She stared at the destination.

Bozeman, Montana.

She knew nothing about Montana.

"Why Montana?" she asked. "What's in Montana?"

"Big sky," he said. "Big mountains, wide open spaces." He pointed to the ticket. "That will take you there. I expect to see some great pictures when you return."

"Okay," she said, picking up the ticket.

She looked back at him. "This is incredibly generous."

"Two more things," he said, shrugging her comment aside. "That bag, over by the door, is yours. Take it with you."

She looked at the expensive dark brown leather suitcase by the door which she hadn't noticed before and her eyes widened.

"Wow," she said. "Thank you."

"The second thing," he said, "Don't make any hotel reservations, or invite anyone else to join you."

She wrinkled her forehead as she looked at him. "Why not?"

"I've made other arrangements. I have a man and a driver who will meet you at the airport and take you to your private lodging. This is a personal retreat, just for you. No one else."

"You don't have to go to all that trouble," she said. "I can book my own room."

"Just follow my instructions," His voice turned stern.

"Enjoy your trip, but no hotels on your own, and no companions."

He was acting strange. Intense, stern, generous.

"You have a relaxing, private place to stay. My surprise, just for you. No company," he said. "Promise."

"Yes, okay," she agreed.

He was being generous, and his conditions weren't a big deal.

She'd take books to read. Her "to be read" stack by the bed had grown so tall she'd moved it to the floor, where it had continued to grow until now it looked ready to topple over.

A weekend with nothing she had to do sounded good. Instead of her usual routine of crossing off her to do lists and never getting everything done.

"I'm going to be out of touch this weekend, but you have everything you need. All arrangements have been made. The messaging service will handle calls, and I've already turned it on for this afternoon. So, you can take off early. There's nothing more that needs to be done today."

Emma was ready to argue with him. She knew exactly what needed to be done today and next week.

He held up a hand to stop her, before she could speak. "The world won't end if we both take the weekend off, and I'm sure you have a lot to do before you fly out."

"All right," Emma said. She glanced down at her desk calendar where projects and due dates were listed, some in black ink, some in red.

A small planner in her purse corresponded with this calendar.

If she didn't have to work on her vacation, she wouldn't need to pack her planner.

It might be kind of nice not to need to look at it until she got back.

"You can catch up on everything back here in the office, after your holiday."

"I was in the middle of typing the letter to -"

"Leave it," he interrupted. "Just as it is."

How strange.

It wasn't like her to leave a task unfinished.

"Okay." Still adjusting to the change in her usually quiet, boring job, she stood to get her purse and her coat, leaving the letter as it was.

She reached for her dirty coffee cup with the yellow happy face on it that said 'smile.'

She needed to take it into the kitchen and wash it.

"Janitorial service can get that," he said. "I pay them enough." His usual tone was back, along with his attitude toward money. He made plenty and made sure everyone knew it.

She wondered, not for the first time, how much he made.

As she went over to the leather suitcase and bent down to pick it up, giving it a closer look, she noted how expensive it had to be.

The leather was soft in her hand. This was one thing she wouldn't have bought for herself.

Wealthy people were so different from the blue collar and white-collar people she'd grown up with. Hard workers all.

'Finish what you start,' her dad always said. Those words stuck with her now.

Walking away from unfinished work wasn't easy. Even if her boss said the letter could wait.

He watched her in silence. Whatever was going on in his thoughts, he wasn't sharing.

Holding the suitcase, she paused by the door. "Thank you again for the birthday gifts," she said. "I appreciate them."

"You're welcome, my dear," he gave her a great big smile. "Have a happy birthday."

Smiling back, she then turned and went out, closing the door behind her.

Her birthday was two weeks away. She'd be back by then and could still celebrate the real day with her noisy family, at the old homestead which had been in her family for three generations. A favorite cake, and usually home-made ice-cream, was the tradition which her grandma had begun.

She always had strawberry cake with buttercream icing and strawberries on top along with strawberry ice-cream.

Grandpa Smith used to say she would turn into a strawberry one day, which had always made her giggle.

He'd been gone for seven years, passing just before she'd gotten her driver's license. She regretted that he'd missed seeing her drive her first car, or graduate high school. When her birthday came around, she always thought of her grandpa.

Emma knew her mother would prepare her favorite meal, as she did for each of her three children on their birthdays. That too was a family tradition.

Evan, her oldest brother, would request coconut cake with coconut icing and didn't care what ice cream flavor went with it. Ernest would ask for carrot cake with crème cheese icing and vanilla ice-cream.

Never store bought, the family birthday cakes were

made just the way Emma's grandmother had made them, from scratch.

Emma wouldn't have missed a family birthday celebration for the world. Especially her own. She'd be back home in time. This was a quick trip, like her boss said, a short, restful vacation.

She'd never taken a vacation or stayed out of town for even one night by herself.

Strange how the birthday gift was now shifting her whole world, making her pivot.

She was a planner, not a fly by the seat of your pants kind of woman.

On her way home, she would already be making lists in her head of what she needed to do before leaving. Unlike her office job, she would not be leaving things undone at home.

Emma made it to her car, a small white Toyota Corolla with beige seats, unlocked it, placed her purse and the new suitcase on the passenger seat and then slid behind the wheel.

Briefly, she thought of calling her mother, but it was always best not to do that while driving.

Her mother would make a huge fuss about her only daughter traveling alone to another state.

No one could make such a fuss as Olivia Smith when she latched onto something.

The boys could do just about anything, but let Emma go off on her own and her mother would start fussing.

When she went off to college, her experience had been different from her brothers. Evan and Ernie simply piled their stuff into their cars when it was time and headed off alone. No fuss had been made, though their mother kept dabbing at her eyes with a tissue.

Setting Emma up in the college dorm, her parents had driven her and carried things into her new room before taking her out to dinner.

For Jim Smith, her father, this was one way he shown that he loved her. He'd worked hard to provide for them and treating her to dinner was his way of sending her off with love. She always valued time with her father, though her mother took up most of her attention, as had always been the way.

College expanded Emma's world, loosening her mother's reach and control, though getting a degree in women's studies landed Emma in classrooms of mostly women, another kind of isolation.

She hadn't thought through what kind of job she might get afterward and had been lucky to land her job at the law office of Clement Oakley Esquire, in Dayton, Ohio.

As she hurried home to catch up on laundry and start packing, she decided to put off telling her parents about the trip until she'd done all her laundry and packed her bags.

She knew her mother would be on the phone for at least an hour, no matter how much Emma needed to do to get ready.

She also wanted to bask in her excited feelings about the trip, before anything negative was said about her going.

Mother would be negative.

She pushed thoughts of her mother aside.

What an amazing day this had turned out to be!

Emma couldn't believe how lucky she was. These kinds of things never happened to her, but now they had!

Finally in her pajamas and sitting in bed, under a warm quilt her grandmother had made, she dialed her mother.

Her mother picked up. "Hello? Emma? Is everything all right?"

"Yes, mom, everything is fine."

"You don't usually call this late."

"I've been busy since I got off work and now, I finally have a minute," Emma said.

"What's going on?" her mother said.

"My boss gave me a really nice birthday gift today."

"It's not your birthday yet," her mother said. "Did he get the date wrong?"

"I didn't ask that. He surprised me. You'll never guess what he gave me."

"What did he give you?"

"A trip to Montana."

"A what? That's an expensive gift!"

"And a new leather suitcase."

"It would have been better if he had given you a bonus."

Of course, mother would say that. She's always about money.

"Well, he didn't, so I'm going to enjoy what he gave me."

"Why such an extravagant gift? And when is this trip?"

"I fly out Monday."

"You won't be here on your birthday."

"I'll be back before then."

"Have him reschedule."

"No. He's shutting down the office for the weekend and given me time off. I can't ask him to reschedule."

"Now, think, Emma," her mother said with that tone Emma disliked. "This doesn't give either of your brothers enough time to arrange to accompany you. You should be more considerate of your brothers."

There it was. So predictable.

"I'm not going to ask either of them to go with me."

Asking one of her brothers to go with her was ridiculous. Even if she'd wanted to, which she didn't.

They both had jobs and girlfriends. Lives of their own.

"I don't like the idea of you flying alone."

"Mom, I'll be on a plane full of people. And I don't need a babysitter, I'm a grown woman."

"Is this boss of yours going with you?" Her mother's voice took on a suspicious tone.

"No. This is a vacation just for me. A retreat. And no one else is invited."

"Well." Her mother huffed. "You needn't be rude about it."

She never likes it when I put up a boundary of any kind.
I really need a vacation from her.

"I'm just stating a fact, mother," Emma said.

Usually stating a fact did not get you into trouble. Something she'd learned working for an attorney.

"Mr. Oakley set this up as a private retreat vacation."

"I don't like it," her mother said.

"Well, I'm excited about the trip," Emma said. "And I do need a vacation. So, I'm going to enjoy it."

"Are you coming over, before you leave?" her mother asked. "I'll fix dinner and invite your brothers."

"Not for dinner," Emma said. "But I could drop by on my way to the bank tomorrow, to see you and dad."

The last thing she was going to do was endure a family dinner with all four of them expressing their opinions on her upcoming trip.

"I've got to get some sleep, mom. It's been a long day."

"Well, then I'll see you tomorrow. We'll talk about this again. Good night."

"Good night."

Emma hung up the phone, vowing not to spend any

more time than necessary visiting her parents, since her mother wasn't supportive of her vacation and happy for her.

Why can't she be happy for me?

I really need a vacation from the negativity.

* * *

Monday, Emma boarded the plane, clutching the paper ticket with excitement. She'd printed it out as a keepsake. The ticket eventually would go into her memory box, where she collected things to make a scrapbook.

On the plane, she sat in the aisle seat, wishing she had the window seat.

Maybe the plane won't be full, and I can switch seats.

A tall man stood in the aisle clearing his throat to get her attention. "I have the seat next to you," he said.

"Sorry," she blushed, and stood, to step into the aisle.

"No problem," he said. He moved into the seat and sat.

A mother, wrestling a baby, sat in the seat across the aisle from Emma. She pulled out a bottle to feed the baby.

Emma hadn't realized you could fly with babies, but the mother acted as if this was nothing unusual.

A large man appeared next to Emma and pointed to the window seat, indicating he needed to be there. She and the man next to her stood and moved out to let him in. Once he was seated, she wondered how he'd squeezed into his seat.

The plane took off, and Emma wished again that she had the window seat.

The tall man next to her was having to lean her way because the other man took up more room than his seat allowed, and he'd put the arm rest up to give him more room which put him over onto the middle seat more. Neither man looked comfortable.

"Close quarters," the man next to her said, "We might as well get to know each other." He held out his hand with a smile. "Brett Collier."

"Emma Smith," she said, reaching to shake his hand.

They shook and smiled at each other.

"Sardines," the large man said. "They squeeze us in here like sardines." He turned his head away from them and looked out the window.

Guess he's not interested in introducing himself or making much conversation, Emma thought. Which was fine with her.

"Headed to Bozeman?" Brett asked. "Or beyond?"

"Bozeman," she said.

"Me too," he said. "Work trip."

It was a one-way flight, so it made sense that they were headed to the same place.

"What do you do?" she asked.

"I'm an analyst," he said. "And you?"

"Just a secretary," she said.

Before they could speak further, her phone rang, and she looked to see who was calling.

Mother.

She answered. "Hello, mom," she said. "The plane is getting ready to take off, so I have to put my phone in airplane mode."

"Be safe," her mother said. "Call me as soon as you land."

"Yes, I will," Emma said. "Love you. Bye."

"Love you. Bye," her mother said.

Emma hung up the phone then set it on airplane mode.

"Mothers," Brett said. "They always worry."

"True," she said. "Mine worries so much that she expects a phone call from me every day."

"Guilts you if you don't, I'm guessing," he said.

"Yep," she gave a nod. "Sure does."

It wasn't going to be much of a retreat if she had to call her mother every day. She'd already decided she wouldn't be. Once her mother knew she'd arrived at the retreat safely, Emma would take a break from the daily calls and turn off her phone.

She would curl up with a good book and order in dinner.

The flight attendant handed Emma a pair of ear buds.

"Thank you," Emma said. She hooked them to the plug at her seat and selected a music compilation of soft piano music to listen to.

Closing her eyes, she tried to tune out everything, and mostly succeeded as she relaxed to the music.

Brett tapped her shoulder when the flight attendant stopped to ask if they wanted drinks and snacks.

Emma took off her earbuds and accepted a cranberry juice, and a biscuit cookie.

She drank half the juice before closing her eyes again to listen to the music, forgetting the cookie.

She was tired as she'd hardly had any sleep last night, between the last phone call with her mother right before bed, which had gone on longer than an hour and had felt like an interrogation, and her excitement about the trip.

Nothing her mother had said had changed Emma's enthusiasm. If anything, it made her want to get away even more.

She'd done a quick search on the internet for Montana, before she'd called her mother, and was hoping to see the beautiful scenery and wildlife.

Emma dozed, finally able to relax enough to do so.

A message that the plane would be landing came over the speakers, so she put away the earbuds.

Brent was talking to the man by the window about football. He turned to her and said, "Better finish your juice and put your tray table up."

Realizing he was right; she finished her juice and gave the cup to the attendant coming down the aisle to collect trash. She tucked the cookie in her purse.

Brett gave her a smile but said nothing.

She was curious about him and would have asked him questions, but she didn't want him to know she'd be alone in Montana.

It wasn't wise to let strangers know she was traveling alone. Her mother had lectured her, and it was one thing she agreed with her mother on.

If she didn't call her mother the minute the plane landed, her phone would start ringing.

So, she waited to turn it back on.

The plane landed, and then she exited the plane, entered the airport, and headed for the baggage carousel.

Brett followed her off the plane, and headed for the baggage claim area as well, but that didn't feel creepy. Just friendly.

He stopped beside her, and they waited for their bags.

When her two bags came around, he helped her by lifting each one off the carousel and sitting it on the floor, beside her.

Her big backpack looked like it didn't belong with the nice leather suitcase.

"Where are you headed?" Brett asked. "Maybe we could share a taxi."

He was probably only trying to save money, but she had to tell him no.

"Thanks, but I already have a ride," she said, her attention on turning her phone back on.

"Maybe we could get together later," he said, and she looked up at him. "For coffee or breakfast. May I have your number?"

Her mother's messages were now coming through, one after the other.

Emma frowned.

Five of them. This is ridiculous.

The warnings her mother had given her were in her mind as she stood beside the handsome man who wanted her number.

He was really a neighbor from the plane, not a guy who approached her from out of the blue. Should she say yes?

Before she could answer, a man approached her from behind. "Miss Emma Smith?"

"Yes," she turned to face the man with the deep voice, wondering if he was the driver Mr. Oakley had hired.

He was tall, six foot five to her five foot six and he stood towering over her.

Broad-shouldered with dark hair showing traces of gray, he appeared strong and fit for his age.

She looked at his crooked nose wondering if his nose had been broken at some point.

While she checked him out, he sent Brett a look which made him back away.

"Enjoy Montana," Brett said with a wave.

We won't be exchanging phone numbers.

Emma was a little disappointed.

She'd been tempted to meet him for coffee, to see if anything further was possible, despite her mother's warnings.

But she needed to get on with her vacation and get that

much-needed rest and relaxation. Alone. As Mr. Oakley had made her promise.

She was tired after the flight, not ready for a date. Even a simple coffee date.

The tall man moved with a smoothness she wouldn't have expected in such a muscle-bound man, capturing her attention away from Brett, and any regrets she might now have.

He held his hand out. "Nathan Smalls," he said. "Your boss, Clement Oakley, sent me. I'll drop you at your lodging."

She grinned.

Small he was not.

Emma reached out her hand out to shake his. "Emma," she said, though he already knew that.

"Yes, ma'am," he smiled at her as they shook, then he picked up her bags. "Ready?" he asked.

Emma nodded and began to walk beside Mr. Smalls, who made her feel small, next to him.

She dialed her mother as they walked.

"Hey mom," she said, the minute her mother picked up. "I'm at the airport and my driver is here, so we're heading to my lodging next. I'll call you when we get there."

For a change, she hadn't let her mother get a word in

"I'm glad you made it safely," her mother said. "How was your flight?"

"Tell you later. Got to go." Emma hung up her phone.

Mother wouldn't like that.

Emma hurried to keep up with Mr. Smalls who wasn't moving slow and set her phone to vibrate.

They left the airport area, with him looking around, as if scanning for trouble.

What's he looking for?

She found herself looking where he was looking, to spot who, or what he was looking for.

His smile had fled, replaced by seriousness that made him look intimidating. Clearly, he was in work mode.

Outside, she thought he'd hail a taxi as he headed toward the taxi stand, but instead, a long dark limo pulled up in front of him and he guided her toward it.

That must be our ride. She glanced at him.

He acts like he's trying to protect me. But why? I'm no celebrity with a bodyguard and limo. I'm just Emma. This whole thing is strange.

This trip is unexpected, hard to get used to, and strange.

He guided her to the limo, waited as she got in, said something to the driver which she couldn't hear, then got in beside her, shutting the door.

Automatic locks clicked down.

She could feel her phone vibrating in her purse which sat on her lap.

Putting it on the seat next to her, she could see many messages coming in from her mother and chose to ignore them. When she got to her destination, then she would call her mother and let her know where she was.

Mr. Smalls was watching the rearview mirror and the driver.

I'm supposed to be enjoying this limo ride. Mr. Oakley meant this as a treat, some pampering for me.

She took in the limo, trying to enjoy the new experience.

A rental car would've been fine. Then I'd have a vehicle to drive around.

What if my "private lodging" is out in the sticks, with no way to get around?

She wasn't used to fancy on her brown bag lunch

budget. Eating out anywhere was a treat. Sometimes her boss would order in a working lunch from a nice restaurant, often Italian.

Emma glanced around the interior of the dark limo and ran her hand across the soft black leather upholstery.

How easy it would be to sink into this seat and fall asleep. How tempting.

She was tired, and badly needed sleep, but a nap wasn't going to happen until after she reached her destination and was safely in her room. She needed to see where she was going.

Which was where, exactly?

She still had no idea. And that gave her an odd feeling.

"Where, exactly, are we headed?" she asked Nathan.

Surely, he can tell me now.

He was frowning at his phone as he read a text message. He didn't answer her, but texted the person on the phone back, the frown not leaving his face.

Whoever is texting him is not making him happy.

She pulled out her phone to call Mr. Oakley and thank him again for the trip.

Maybe he'd finally tell her where she'd be staying.

She started to look up his number. In her peripheral vision she saw Mr. Smalls whole demeanor change.

He'd called someone on his cell phone, and when they picked up, said, "what happened," in a quiet voice before he sat listening, still as a stone. The tension in his body clear.

Something is wrong.

She glanced down at her phone, at Mr. Oakley's number, ready to push dial, and then pushed it and lifted the phone to her ear.

Mr. Smalls said, "When did it happen?"

He listened again. "Thanks, mate," he said, hung up and turned to face her. "Change of plans."

The ringing phone at her ear went to voice mail and she heard her boss say to leave a message.

"What?" She asked Mr. Smalls, confused. "What do you mean?"

Mr. Smalls grabbed her cell phone out of her hand. "Who are you calling?"

"Mr. Oakley," she said.

"Damn it." He disconnected the call.

Why is he so upset?

He clenched his fist around her phone, lowered his window and tossed her phone out the window.

"Hey!" she yelled as her phone went flying away from the limo. "That was mine!"

What the hell?

Closing the window, glancing briefly at the limo driver who was watching them in the rearview mirror and listening, Mr. Smalls turned to face her.

"Your boss is dead," he spoke, his voice low and calm.

She gasped.

Mr. Oakley dead?

The limo driver met her wide eyes in the rear-view mirror.

Chapter Two

Brett Collier enjoyed sitting next to the pretty woman named Emma Smith on the plane.

She clearly wasn't an experienced flier, and he'd always enjoyed helping pretty women. By the time they'd landed, he'd wondered if she would allow him to treat her to coffee.

A getting to know you date, or a pre-date, whichever one she would choose.

Emma had an innocence about her, rare in a female her age, that he found attractive. It made him feel protective of her as he watched a man approach her in the airport.

She hadn't said anything about meeting someone.

Brett, far from shy, stayed quiet as he took in the man approaching Emma, who from her reaction, must have been expecting someone to meet her.

Analyzing intel was one thing he did well, quietly being aware of his surroundings and the people interacting around him was another.

He was a behavioral specialist, and just as interested in

observing people in person as he was interested in learning data about them.

Nathan Smalls had the size and bearing of a boxer or some other type of fighter, and the sort of energy that went with it.

As he watched the two of them walk away, though he would have enjoyed getting to know Emma further, he was glad she wouldn't be alone in a city she'd never been in before.

She was being looked after, and their paths would likely never cross again.

This was a work trip for him.

Something made him watch her all the way to the limo, until she got in, making sure all was well, before he got his own ride, which would go on his expense account.

It was a habit, making sure of things, hanging out longer than most people would have.

The something which made him hang back must not have been his intuition this time, but more than likely came from too much time spent analyzing people with bad intentions.

That practice could make you see bad intentions everywhere.

He told himself she was fine. Would be fine.

A DEA agent, he was part of the Rocky Mountain Field Division, covering Colorado, Utah, Wyoming, and Montana. He'd traveled to Montana for meetings in Bozeman and Billings to share what intel he'd discovered on the Sinaloa cartel operating in the area.

Operations needed the information to help with planning. He would meet with them tomorrow afternoon in the first meeting and then the following day in Billings.

Though he would have enjoyed coffee with Emma tomorrow morning, it wasn't to be.

Such was life as a DEA agent.

Instead, he would order room service for breakfast and enjoy his quiet room before he had to be at work in the early afternoon. Then he'd find a good steak somewhere for dinner and rest tomorrow night before he drove his rental car to Billings.

At best, he would only have been able to have coffee, and maybe dinner, with Emma before he had to leave.

If she were even interested in a date.

Pushing her from his mind, he put his thoughts back on work as he headed to his hotel.

Inside the dark limo, Mr. Smalls took Emma's hand and squeezed it. "Shh," he spoke low. "We have an audience. I need you to stay calm."

She had a floating feeling, like she'd drifted into a dream. The beginnings of a nightmare.

Mr. Oakley couldn't be dead.

On Friday, before he sent her home early, he was very much alive.

She'd just heard his voice on his voice mail, telling her to leave a message, as if he was right there. He'd sounded alive on the phone.

My phone!

"Why did you throw my phone out the window?" She yanked her hand back, as if his hand would burn her, while staring at the hand which had just thrown her phone out the window.

"Calm down," he said. "We don't know who has his phone, and you can be tracked with yours," he said.

"Tracked?" she frowned.

What does he mean I can be tracked?

"Your vacation has been compromised," Mr. Smalls continued talking low, while she stared at him.

"You can't stay in Bozeman. It's on your ticket. That's where they'll look."

"My ticket?" she asked him, completely confused.

"Your plane ticket. Flight information is easy to obtain," he said. "You can't stay in Bozeman. You're traceable here. We're leaving."

"Leaving?" frustration filled her. "I just got here. Now where are we going?"

He placed one finger on her lips. "Shh." He gestured his head toward the limo driver. "It's imperative no one knows where we're going."

She kept her voice low. "Won't the limo driver know?"

"No."

He spoke to the limo driver, giving him a new address.

The limo driver nodded.

"Are we going to pick up a rental car?" she spoke low.

Nathan shook his head, giving her a frown.

He probably wanted her to stop asking questions.

But she had so many.

Unable to stop herself, she asked another. "How far is it?"

She had to know where he was taking her.

Her boss knew Mr. Smalls, but she didn't. He was a stranger to her, and now he was the only one in Montana who knew where she was, other than the limo driver.

All her mother's repeated warnings about strangers and traveling alone came back to her.

Who is Nathan Smalls, really? How does Mr. Oakley know him?

She caught herself. *Did, not does. Mr. Oakley is dead.*

She was still having trouble adjusting to that fact.

Mr. Oakley would have told her to 'stick to the facts.' She'd heard him say it a million times to clients.

But what were those facts?

How had Mr. Oakley died? And when exactly?

Who had killed him? And why?

She had a bad feeling in her gut. So many questions filled her head. Already tired, now she was confused as well.

Just what the hell is going on?

Mr. Smalls wasn't talking.

She stared at him, wishing he would tell her something. Anything.

Finally, he held out two fingers, low enough the limo driver couldn't see.

She copied his movement, and whispered, "hours?"

He nodded.

So. Two hours away. What city is two hours away?

She couldn't even guess.

The little she knew about Montana had centered around Bozeman, because that's where she was supposedly staying. It was the only place she'd looked up. She'd been so busy packing and getting ready to go out of town, there hadn't been time.

Now she wasn't even going to be there, but instead would be two hours away. In which direction?

She needed to know what had happened to Mr. Oakley.

"What happened to my boss?" she whispered.

It didn't seem possible that he was dead. She'd last

spoken to him, three days ago, before going home early, taking her new suitcase and her airline ticket.

He'd been very much alive then.

An active man, he played golf on Saturdays and tennis on Sundays. He was in good health.

But now he was dead.

"Not now," Nathan said low.

"Was he killed?"

"We'll talk about it later."

She pursed her lips, keeping her thoughts to herself.

Yes, we will. I want to know what my boss has gotten me into. Who killed him. And why I'm now on the run, instead of on the restful vacation I'd been promised.

She crossed her arms and scowled at Nathan Smalls but kept her thoughts to herself.

I'm on the run with a man I just met, know nothing about, going somewhere I don't know. Without my phone.

Mother will be having fits right about now. It will take her a while to calm down and for anyone to figure out I'm missing.

They won't even have a hotel to call because where I was to be staying was a secret.

"This is crazy!" Scowling, she whispered at him.

Just what has Mr. Clement Oakley Esquire gotten me into?

The birthday gift no longer felt like a gift.

He sent me out of town.

The realization left a bad feeling in the pit of her stomach which now growled.

Why had he sent me out of town? What was he involved in?

His words came back to her.

He'd said 'getaway.' Then corrected himself. That must have been a slip of the tongue.

Get away from what?

It felt like she'd stepped into one of those television shows with plots, bad guys, and a detective who had to figure everything out.

Why would anyone come after me?

I'm just the secretary.

She stared out the window at scenery she barely noted.

It was hard to appreciate scenery when you were on the run.

* * *

The driver pulled over where Mr. Smalls told him to stop.

After paying the driver and collecting her bags, they started walking toward an old motel.

Emma wrinkled her nose.

I hope we aren't staying here.

"Come on," he said, once the driver pulled away, and he started walking past the hotel and down a street that ran behind it.

They walked for two blocks until he stopped on the corner of the sidewalk and looked both ways.

She looked with him, wondering what he was looking for.

No traffic passed.

Maybe that was what he was watching for, as he then turned and walked up toward a rickety old wooden house with faded paint and a matching garage that stood on the corner lot.

He moved to the garage and set her bags down. Then he

reached for the garage door handle. Once he'd opened it, he gestured to her to step inside.

When she did, he took her bags, followed her in and put the garage door back down again behind them.

An old white Ford truck with some rust, sat inside. He opened the truck door, felt above the visor and under the floor mat, before coming up with the keys.

"Get in," he said.

She got in the passenger side.

"Give me your driver's license and anything else with your name on it," he said.

"Why?" She frowned at him.

"You're going under cover, darlin'," he said. "What's your middle name?"

"Pearl."

"Emma Pearl Smith, you are now Pearl Hays," he said. "Do not use your real name for anything, until we know for certain that you are safe."

She didn't like this. Reluctantly she got her wallet and removed her driver's license, credit cards, and even her library card with her name on it. She included the plane ticket she'd printed out.

Once she handed them all to him, he pulled a padded envelope from a drawer beneath the workshop, and a permanent magic marker.

He handed them to her. "Write your home address on this," he said. "We'll mail them, and they'll be waiting for you when you're able to go home again."

I'll send them to mother and dad. Then they'll know something has happened to me. They might even know from the postage mark where it was mailed from and what time I was here.

He stepped inside, was gone less than five minutes, and came back carrying a bag full of stuff.

She wondered what was in the bag.

He put the bag in the truck, reached inside and pulled out several stamps.

"Put these on and we'll mail them on the way out of town."

She wrote down her parents address on the envelope and added her name at the top.

He wouldn't know the difference, unless he took the time to read her driver's license, and he wouldn't see that once the package was sealed.

He yanked the baggage tickets off her two bags, threw them into a trash can, and then reached in to start the truck. He put her bags in the truck and then went back to open the garage door again.

Everything in the garage was of an age. There was no garage door opener other than Mr. Smalls.

Emma sealed the envelope and added the stamps. She placed it on her lap. With her driver's license inside the sealed envelope, he wouldn't know what she'd done.

She'd left her parents one clue.

They could figure out where she was today, even if they didn't know where she would be tomorrow.

Even she didn't know where she would be tomorrow.

I hope I can send them another clue, later.

He pulled the door open, climbed into the truck, and then backed it out of the garage onto the driveway. Then he got out and closed the garage door again with a sense of urgency.

This, more than anything else, made her nervous. He looked capable of defending himself. If this big guy was nervous, how could she not be?

Once they were both in the truck, driving away, he asked "What's your name?"

She frowned at him. He knew her name.

"Your new name. Practice," he said, then repeated, "What's your name?"

"Pearl Hays," she said.

"Good girl," he said. "Remember that. And you can call me Nathan. Mr. Smalls sounds like you're addressing your teacher, and we need to appear to be together."

"Fine," she said. Though nothing about this situation was fine. It was like something from a movie she didn't want to be in.

"Is Nathan Smalls your real name?" she asked.

"One of them," he said.

What's that supposed to mean?

He drove to the post office and parked. "Don't talk to anyone, just drop it off," he said.

She nodded.

He waited while she walked the envelope up to the drop off box and dropped it in.

If anything happens to me, mother and dad will know I was just here, and something has gone wrong.

She kept hugging that thought to herself as she walked back to his truck. It made her feel better to know what she'd done. Taken some action and not been just a victim of fate.

Once she got in the truck, he said, "Done?"

"Yes," she answered, and he put the truck in reverse.

They didn't speak again for about a half hour.

Then every half hour he asked again what her name was.

She closed her eyes and laid her head back against the headrest, tired of it all. Tired and just wanting to go home to see her family again. Even her frustrating mother.

* * *

In Montana, a DEA task force had formed, and Brett Collier was a part of it.

Rocky Mountain HIDTA, a counter narcotics program administered by the ONDCP office of national drug control to directly support law enforcement agencies at the federal, state, local, and tribal levels had put together twenty-eight individual task forces totaling more than one hundred thirty agencies in Colorado, Utah, Wyoming, and Montana.

Sharing intel between these areas was essential once it was gathered and to this task Brett gave his all.

Today he was bringing information to local law enforcement in Bozeman and Billings.

The meeting was to discuss cartel activity in Montana as well as a plan of action for taking down the cartel. This time it would be two-fold.

James Arnold, the special agent in charge (SAC) managing the task force, would update local law enforcement about the two-pronged plan they would put into place.

With him, he had FBI agent Don Loftus, DEA agents Eldon Marks and Scott Baker, and a third, Brett Collier, who'd flown into Bozeman.

Sheriff Colt was there with two deputy's, Craig Brown and Morris Cooper, and five police officers from Billings, Lieutenant Rod Kelly, Chad Brooks, Austin Foster, Trevor Hill, and Charles O'Malley. The room was crowded as they all filed in to take their seats.

The task force was a mix of state and local officers, all deputized as federal drug agents extending their jurisdiction so that they could perform the same functions as federal agents. This removed the issue of whose jurisdiction something happened in and allowed them all to work together with the shared goal of taking the cartel down in the western United States.

Once they were seated, James Arnold began to speak. "We have a multi-pronged approach to taking down the cartels here in Montana. As you know, we have semis coming into the area which bring drugs. Some are packaged for delivery, and some are mobile drug labs which produce as they travel."

"In the past, when we've seized one of their semis, they just replace it with a new one. It makes hardly a dent in their multi-billion-dollar operation. No matter how much we seize, they can make more."

Heads were nodding. This was something they all knew.

"Learning this," he continued. "We then turned to watching the semis and waiting, so that instead of taking a semi out of commission, we could focus on the dealers who were picking up the drugs and the users who were using them. But arresting them hasn't been enough."

It was something they all agreed on, and many had voiced their frustrations about how the war on drugs hadn't been going well. It seemed an unending and uphill battle. Arrests were a quick and temporary solution which could last less than a week before another semi was in the area and more dealers were lined up to sell.

"One prong, 'Operation Cash Out', which special agent Collier has been focusing on, is a focus on the money side of cartel operations, to hit them where it hurts the most. We now have two hundred money service businesses in this operation, and we are focused on the money coming in and going out. This will lead to IRS criminal investigations and closing many of the money pipelines."

All eyes followed him as he took up a black marker and using a white board, drew out a rough sketch of the roads to and from Billings and the long stretches of roads between other towns and Billings. Also included were the reservation lands and the roads in and out of the reservation.

"Here are the points we'll want to watch," he said as he turned to face them.

He tapped one road which ran between Billings, Montana and Cody Wyoming.

"We've been undercover monitoring route 120 here between Billings and Cody at the entry points to each city for the past three months, surveilling semi-trucks and making note of tag numbers."

Brett watched him, wondering if there was anyone in the room who wasn't aware of this already. He wished the SAC would get on with the recap and to the point where Brett could give them the new information he had.

The SAC tapped the whiteboard, "Our three-month surveillance has turned up a pattern, here. And we want to disrupt that pattern. Brett Collier is a DEA analyst and our intel guy. Brett, tell us what you've learned."

Brett stood and spoke, getting straight to the points he had to make. "Most of the trucks are registered to the same guy. Jean Palafox, who is a member of the Sinaloa cartel. And we have intel on this truck. We've been able to locate his financial transactions and have been watching them for irregularities and patterns."

Most people had at least one pattern even if they were trying not to. If you watched them long enough you would see it. This was what Brett lived for, finding patterns in people who were trying to hide themselves or their actions.

"He's squirrelly, but he too has a pattern."

He wrote a tag number on the whiteboard, and then

pointed to it. "We have intel that this truck has unloaded on the reservation more than once. Money patterns on Palafox match the pattern of the truck deliveries. We want to take this one down, before the semi unloads again, now that we have enough info for the IRS to go after him on the money."

"Two prong," Sheriff Colt said. "I like it."

* * *

The task force now hidden along the highway had good intel on the white semi-truck that was coming and were ready to take it down. Word had spread from Wyoming up to the men who were waiting for it to show, and they knew exactly where it was and where they would intercept it.

Not too close to the city and civilians, because cartel members always carried heavy guns and would shoot anyone nearby them without hesitation.

Out here on that long stretch of road there would be no innocent bystanders.

Sheriff Colt, Deputy Brown and Deputy Morris were ready, along with Scott Baker from the DEA, and Lieutenant Rod Baker and Austin Foster from the Billings police department.

Recently a black van had been driving just enough back that it appeared not to be driving with the semi, but mirroring its movements, the likelihood was that it was.

The van bore watching.

Sheriff Colt did not like darkened windows on vans or other vehicles. It was too hard to see the dangers waiting inside, turning a simple traffic pull-over into a death trap for law enforcement officers.

Six LEO's on a stakeout might have seemed like overkill

to some, but when dealing with the cartels, more manpower was smarter than less.

Emma and Mr. Smalls were outside the city limits of Billings, Montana, two hours from Bozeman, when a white semi behind them started speeding up, acting as if the driver wanted to run them off the road.

Nathan sped up as the semi-truck almost rammed them.

Suddenly a black van with dark windows raced around from behind the semi into the lane next to them.

"Where the hell did he come from?" Nathan muttered.

Emma looked over her shoulder at the black van as it sped up beside them.

Once it was beside them, the side door began to slide open.

"Damn it! The cartel found us," Nathan said. He pushed the gas pedal to the floor, trying to outrun them, but the van kept pace beside him.

"Cartel?" Emma squeaked out, her frightened voice coming out high pitched.

As the van kept pace with their truck, the van door slid open and two men with big guns leaned out, taking aim.

"Get down!" Nathan shouted as the men pointed their guns at Emma ready to shoot.

Emma screamed and momentarily froze.

"On the floor! Now!" Nathan yelled.

Emma jammed the button that unlocked her seatbelt, forced her way out of it, and slid down to the floor beneath her seat. She crouched, as small as she could make herself.

The men fired their guns, the sounds loud.

She screamed again in terror.

"Stay down!" Nathan shouted at her.

Chapter Three

Destry Walsh fed and watered his horse, Arrow, and his border collie, Scout, then gave instructions to his neighbor, Mac, who helped on the small ranch when Destry worked long shifts at the Billings Clinic.

It was a bit of a drive, but Destry had no taste for city living.

He had built the ranch house on newly developed land between Billings, Montana and Cody, Wyoming and he couldn't have been happier with his new home.

As he got in his truck to drive to work at the hospital, he wondered again who he might ask to go to the 4th of July rodeo with him.

Those two tickets would burn a hole in his pocket until he had a companion to take with him.

He hadn't been dating much lately.

How long had it been now?

Mostly he worked at the hospital and took care of his animals and his ranch.

He didn't want to date women he worked with, but he

wasn't sure where else to meet women, when he was so busy.

After he arrived on the floor, which was busier than usual, he got a briefing from the pretty nurse he was replacing before the shift change.

Opal Lessor, a Philippine traveling nurse, was pretty enough to distract him at work so he had to focus when she was near.

But she barely knew him, and the traveling nurses tended not to date, before they moved on to the next nursing job. So, he'd crossed off the idea of asking her out.

They had to work together and didn't need complications to that.

With a shortage of nurses, the Billings Clinic had started hiring traveling nurses so they wouldn't be short staffed.

Destry had been hired as soon as he had applied.

He was a local, born and raised in Greybull, Wyoming, only a few hours from Billings. He had experience and an RN degree.

After his time in Delta Force which included ten surgeries to repair things that had happened to him overseas, he'd left the military, moving on from his spec Ops medic training, which he'd enjoyed, to become an RN in civilian life.

Now he worked at the Billings Clinic helping to save people's lives.

In his time off, before he'd finished building his ranch house, he'd lived in Greybull, with family, helping at a relative's ranch. He'd grown up with horses, enjoyed helping with team roping at local rodeos, and on the ranch, but he'd given up thoughts of sticking with rodeo after 9/11.

Instead, he'd enlisted in the Army, just as his father had

after high school. Destry had gone further than his father, becoming Delta Force, and making the whole family proud.

At heart, he was still a rodeo cowboy and held to the values he'd been raised with.

Every time someone had tried to give him a military nickname, he'd countered with, "Just call me Destry."

Apparently, that was cool enough, and since no one had thought of a better name for him, just Destry he remained.

The name was uncommon enough that he'd only heard it once, in the old west movie 'Destry Rides Again.'

Destry Walsh had stopped his share of bad men, and was an excellent shot, but he now spent his time saving civilian lives who'd been shot. He enjoyed working in the ER, or on the ICU floor where he was working this week.

"Stay down!" Nathan shouted at Emma as bullets ripped through the car.

The car's frame was no protection from the bullets being sprayed as they pierced the metal.

But the men's aim was high. Not low near the floor where she crouched, praying.

Please God, don't let them kill me. Keep me alive. And keep Nathan safe too.

The semi suddenly moved on, fast down the highway, as the men in the van kept shooting.

Nathan punched the gas harder, making the truck go as fast as it could.

Gunshots kept coming, but in the distance, she heard the wail of a siren.

Was it the police?

Please God, let it be the police and help them stop those men.

The siren sounded nearer as the patrol car was moving fast. And suddenly she realized it was more than one siren and raised her head up, her instinct to look.

The police were coming!

Hope filled her.

Emma felt a sudden pain in her left shoulder.

I've been shot.

At the same time Nathan slumped over the steering wheel, giving her no time for the shock of being shot, and making the car spin off the highway.

Oh my God, no!

The car spun onto the embankment at the side of the road, bumping off the highway and then hurtling nose down into a dry rocky ditch.

She banged her head on the window, hard, which dazed her.

"Dammit," Mr. Smalls rasped, and turned his head toward her, but he didn't rise from the steering wheel. "Told you to stay down. Now you're hit."

He's still alive. His voice and breathing sound strange.

"In my left shoulder," she said.

"Not worse, good," He coughed and then rasped again. "Don't give anyone your real name."

"I won't," she said.

"The cartel killed your boss, and now they're after us."

"What?" The news stunned her speechless. Her mind wrestled with grasping it. "I don't understand," she said. "Why?"

"You aren't safe," he rasped again. "Cartels pay people off. You don't know who they have in their pockets." He coughed and it sounded like he was choking. "Don't trust anyone," he rasped out.

It was the last thing she heard before sudden silence and darkness as she blacked out.

* * *

The task force had killed the four gunmen from the cartel, but now they had two victims that needed EMTs pronto.

Sheriff Colt's voice was grim as he radioed it in. He hoped the couple made it. Good thing they were closer to the city where the EMTs might arrive in time.

As he waited, another call came in.

An escaped felon had threatened the woman who sold tacos from her taco truck at a little town toward Cody. He'd stolen her money, and was thought to still be at large in the area, possibly headed to his ex-girlfriend's house.

He and his deputy's had to go.

This still left four men on the scene, and the danger of gunshots had passed. Deputy Brown would update him later and he could follow up on the couple at the hospital.

After a brief word with the DEA man, Sheriff Colt and his deputy both sped off.

* * *

When Emma started to come to, Nathan's words were still running in her mind. She was in danger because the cartel was trying to kill her.

She turned her head from side to side with a moan as her eyes opened to frantically search for the gunmen.

Instead, she saw two EMTs beside her, working on her.

She was on one of those ambulance beds, covered with a blanket.

It was strangely quiet, now that the gunfire had stopped, but those sounds in her head were a memory she hadn't forgotten.

eA part of her listened for more gunfire and her body was tense waiting for another sudden attack.

Pain in her left shoulder made her wince.

The female EMT on her right said, "She's awake," to the other EMT, who then spoke to her. "What's your name, honey?"

She wasn't supposed to give anyone her real name.

What is my new name?

She thought hard and frowned. Then it came to her.

"Pearl," she said. "Hayes."

"That's a pretty name, Pearl," the EMT said. "We couldn't find any ID for you. Maybe you lost your wallet. But don't worry. That happens in accidents sometimes and they turn up later. Right now, we just need to know, are you on any meds that we should be aware of?"

"No," she shook her head slightly noticing the sun setting.

It would be dark soon.

She turned her head to look for Nathan Smalls.

Over her right shoulder, two more EMTs were bent over Mr. Smalls, working on him. His eyes were closed.

She gasped. "Is he alive?"

"Yes," the EMT said. "But you've both been shot. We're taking you to the ER now." She and the man began to roll Emma toward the back of the ambulance.

"She's awake," he called to a policeman who nodded and hurried over. His tag said Deputy Brown.

"I'm Deputy Brown," he said. "What's your name?" He pulled his pen out, ready to write things down.

"Pearl Hayes."

"Where are you from, Pearl?"

"Ohio."

"What brings you here to Montana?"

"Vacation."

"And you're traveling with Mr. Smalls?"

"Yes."

"Can you tell me what happened?"

"Crazy men. Raced up to us in a black van and started shooting at us."

"Do you know them?"

"No." She looked over her shoulder again at Nathan, worried. "They might come back."

"They're not coming back from where they're going," Deputy Brown said. "We got them."

"But if they get away?"

The female EMT placed a hand on her good shoulder, the warmth reassuring. "They're not getting away, honey. They're dead. They can't hurt you now."

"Oh good," Emma closed her eyes, sudden relief relaxing her body.

Her prayers had been answered.

"Thank you," she whispered, suddenly very sleepy.

"She's ready for transport," the male EMT said to the deputy. "The rest of your report will have to wait until the doctor gets that bullet out."

"Roger that," Deputy Brown said. "I'll talk to you soon, Pearl. Hang in there. You're going to be okay."

"Okay," she answered meekly, keeping her eyes closed but wincing again as they were now moving her and the bumpiness on the side of the highway jarred her shoulder, causing pain.

Lifting her up and into the ambulance, was more bumping and pain, and then she heard someone close the back doors.

"Nathan?" she asked, remembering him and worrying.

"He's in the other ambulance, Hun," the female EMT said. "He's on his way to the hospital too."

"Oh good," she said. He'd saved her life, and she didn't want anything bad to happen to him.

The siren began as the ambulance pulled away, and the sound made her head hurt. "Too loud," she murmured.

Then they were at the hospital, the siren had stopped, and they were taking her out of the ambulance again, the EMTs hurrying her inside.

Inside, a doctor looked at her right away, and soon they were putting her under, so that another doctor, a surgeon, could take the bullet out.

* * *

Destry watched the sleeping woman who'd just been brought into the ICU.

She's beautiful.

He listened to the update on her status.

And she'd been shot. She was lucky to be alive.

He read through the notes on her case file to catch up to speed. She'd been shot on the highway, just outside Billings, and lucky for her, had survived.

She'd made it to the ER and been operated on right away. The doctor had been able to remove the bullet, but she'd lost a lot of blood, so she wasn't out of the woods yet.

He glanced back over at her.

What happened to you, darlin'?

They'd have to monitor her close.

Destry would check in on her often as well as watching the readouts the machines she was hooked up to were giving.

Were it not for all the wires and tubes she was hooked to, she could've been an angel sleeping.

He watched her for a few moments, taking her in.

Soft lashes closed against smooth cheeks, and dark blonde hair curtained each side of her face. He noted a dark spot on her hair and bent to look closely.

Blood. We'll need to clean her up after she wakes.

He made a note to remember.

And if he didn't get to do it, hopefully a nurse from another shift would.

* * *

Men were chasing her again, with guns. She tried to run.

Then they started shooting.

Pain radiated through her shoulder, and suddenly she knew she'd been shot.

Beeping noises nearby roused her from the nightmare, and she awakened from her dream. But still, she kept her eyes closed, in fear.

Now they would come again.

Those crazy men would come with their great big guns, and they will find me.

And then they will kill me.

At a certain point, through pain and fear, she heard beeping noises, and machine noises, but no gunshots, and she finally opened her eyes.

She woke in the ICU, instead of a recovery room, hooked to machines and IV lines. There was one in her nose, a bunch in her arms, and sticky things on her chest with wires.

Too many machines and wires and noises.

Drowsy, she went in and out, and would have slept, if there weren't so many noisy machines waking her up, and nurses coming in to do things.

They didn't try talking to her and she kept her eyes closed.

In between dozing, she caught bits of things the nurses said to each other.

"She's so pale," nurse Opal said.

"She lost a lot of blood," a man's calm voice answered, his voice pulling at her, the calmness of his voice keeping her from worrying about losing blood, his voice resonating with something within her.

Mystery man.

Sleepy, she wanted to sleep, but his voice pulled her attention, making her want to open her eyes, to see the man with the wonderful voice.

Emma started to wake, to ask about the blood loss, but the pull to sleep was stronger than the pull of his voice and she dozed again.

Now she just wanted to sleep.

Sleep everything away as if the nightmare had never happened.

The nurses kept checking things and talking to each other, which would wake Emma again, though she slept in between.

As the medicines were eased back, she began to be more awake.

Voices woke her again, and she turned her head to look

at two female nurses whispering near the door, probably so they wouldn't wake her.

The lights were bright. She blinked slowly.

Why is everything in here so bright and noisy? Makes it hard to sleep.

"Good thing our deputies are crack shots," a red headed nurse said. "Took out all four of those killers."

"I don't like guns," a dark-haired nurse with a New Jersey accent said.

"Takes a good shot to kill a killer," the redhead said.

"Out here, our boys learn how to shoot as soon as they're old enough to hold a gun. There's coyotes and livestock to protect. Most of their grandma's know how to shoot just as well."

"I still don't like guns," the other nurse said. "They're dangerous."

"Our well-trained deputies saved her life," the nurse said.

"Well, I'm glad of that. Even if guns do make me nervous."

Emma was glad too.

They looked over at her and realized she was awake and watching them.

"You're finally awake," the redhead said. "That's good."

She came over and checked all the things connected to Emma and the machines. "Your vitals are improving."

She turned again to Emma who was so sleepy it was hard to keep her eyes open.

She closed them.

Not sure how long she'd slept, but she was awakened with a pressing need.

"I need to go," Emma said.

The redheaded nurse picked up a bed pan and brought it over. "I'm Terri," she said. "I can help you use this."

"I can't go in that. I need the restroom."

"No, not right now, we can't let you out of bed with all the meds you have in you. And you've got a pad under you."

Emma reached beneath her with her right hand to feel the pad and felt it crinkle.

"You also have a gunshot wound in your shoulder, beneath that bandage which was just operated on."

"I remember being shot," Emma said.

How could I ever forget?

That nightmare had been running in her sleep like a movie she couldn't turn off.

"The good news is the doctor got the bullet out," Terri said. "Now all you need to do is get better. You'll be sore for a while, but it will heal."

So sleepy still.

It was hard to stay awake even though she needed to.

"Where am I?" she asked.

"Billings Clinic," Terri said.

"Billings?"

"Billings, Montana. You're in ICU, but don't worry. This is a tier one hospital, you're in good hands, and you are doing great."

"Billings Clinic, Montana." Emma repeated. "I've never been to Billings."

"I understand you were traveling here when it happened," Terri said.

Mr. Smalls.

Though groggy still, her memory came back.

They'd been shooting at him too.

"They shot him," she said. "Mr. Smalls."

"You were shot once, but Mr. Smalls was shot many times," Terri said. "He's also in ICU, but he's bad off."

"I want to see him," she said.

The nurse shook her head. "He's in a coma and may never wake up." She gave Emma a sad smile. "I'm sorry about your friend. I'll let the doctor know you're awake now."

Emma didn't want to be awake. She was still sleepy even with the pressure to go.

The nurse noticed and said, "It's okay to sleep. Go on and rest now."

Emma remembered getting on a plane but wasn't sure where.

Or even where home was.

Her memories were fuzzy, going in and out. She was still groggy from the medication they'd used to put her under for the surgery.

At least she knew her name. Her real name.

Emma.

Though she didn't dare tell anybody what it was.

She wanted to go back to a time where she'd never gotten on the plane to Bozeman and none of this had happened.

I was typing a letter at work. Who was it for? I never finished it. That isn't like me.

She frowned.

Teri smiled at her. "Try to rest. The doctor will be in shortly, if he hasn't already left. I'll see if I can catch him."

Pearl felt safe here, and the nurse had a comforting nature, so she closed her eyes again.

She could try to remember more things later. Right now, things hurt, and she was sleepy.

When she woke again, she remembered that she still needed to go, and she told them.

Again, a nurse brought her the bed pan.

"I don't think I can do it in that," she said.

"Well, try."

She did try. With no luck.

Closing her eyes with a frustrated sigh she said, "I can't. But I really need to go."

"We can try again when you're ready," the nurse said.

But the meds had Emma groggy, and she dozed, the hospital sounds and the movements of the nurse fading away.

"I don't know why I can't stay awake," she said.

"It's okay," the nurse said. "Sleep is healing."

* * *

"Who is she really?" Sheriff Colt said as he drummed his fingers on the desk. "Pearl Hayes is not in the database."

"Could her name be made up?" Deputy Craig Brown said. "She had no I.D. on her."

They'd collected her purse, her suitcase, and her backpack, and looked through them all, trying to find out who she was, before storing them to give to her later.

Nothing in any of her belongings told them who she was.

With modern technology it was rare to find no records in any of the databases to match a name.

"At least we know the perps," Lieutenant Rod Kelly said. "Every one of them connected to the Sinaloa cartel each has a record a mile long."

The sheriff's office and the Billings police were working together to learn what had gone down and why cartel members had fired on two seemingly innocent travelers on the highway.

"Wonder what they were moving in that semi?" Lieutenant Kelly said. "It's too bad they got away."

They all knew the men from the task force had been given no other choice. Gunfire on the highways had to be stopped. And even if they had confiscated that truck, the cartel could just send another one to replace it.

"Drugs, weapons, or women," Sheriff Colt said.

"Got the plates," Deputy Brown said. "Wasn't much help."

"I'll keep a man on her room to guard her," Lieutenant Kelly said.

Sheriff Colt nodded. "Good."

"Officer Packer, you're on first," Lieutenant Kelly said.

Levi Packer was a seasoned officer who was neither near retirement, nor a rookie.

"Hopefully she'll wake up soon," Deputy Brown said. "Doesn't sound like Smalls is going to make it."

With nothing else that they could do about the case until one of the two was awoke enough to be questioned, their meeting was at an end.

* * *

When Emma next woke, she realized she'd slept through the day.

It was dark outside the windows now.

She still needed to go, more than ever, and wondered where her nurse was.

On the wall was a whiteboard with a place for the name of the nurse assigned to her today. In plain bold letters it said Destry.

That sounds like a man's name.

Then she saw him in the far corner of the room, near the door. He had his back to her, but she could see dark hair and strong shoulders. He stood typing notes into a computer.

As he turned, she caught her breath.

Handsome with alert brown eyes that lit when he saw her watching him, his face spread into a smile that warmed her to her toes. "You're awake," he said, smiling at her. "I'm Destry, your night shift nurse."

That voice. The one I thought I had dreamed. It was him.

The moment he spoke, the resonation inside her began again.

"Nice to meet you," she spoke low, suddenly shy and blushing. She couldn't let him know her reaction to him and his voice. "I'm Pearl."

Part of her wanted to tell him her real name, didn't want to lie to him. Which made no sense, because she didn't know him.

Though his voice made him sound like she did. Like some part of her recognized him.

But that couldn't be possible. She would have remembered meeting this handsome man.

And his name, Destry, was unforgettable.

Right now, something more pressing pulled her attention.

Chapter Four

Her pressing need reminded her that she had something else to worry about beyond the handsome male nurse who was looking at her with those deep brown eyes.

"Can I get up now?" she asked.

"Not yet," Destry said. "What can I get for you?"

Her cheeks blushed with embarrassment. He was being helpful, but he couldn't help her with this. "I need to go," she said. "Really bad."

He immediately got the bed pan and brought it over to her. "Here you are," he said, placing it on the bed. "I'll help you sit up."

He raised her bed which sat her up but also put more pressure on her bladder.

She made a face.

"Hang on, and I'll help you," he said.

He lifted her up, as if she weighed nothing, and then he slid the bed pan beneath her before she could think about being even more embarrassed.

She was still covered by the sheet and had a hospital

gown on, so he wasn't seeing anything. Still, she was embarrassed.

"I'm going to turn my head and give you some privacy, and then you just go," he spoke in that voice, his tone as if this was the most natural thing to do, and of course she could and would. Not a spec of doubt that she wouldn't.

He had more belief in her than she did.

So, she tried, but with him right there, she just couldn't.

"I don't think I can do this in a bed," she said, "but I really need to go."

"Darlin' I can't help you out of bed yet, but I can get a female nurse to step in," he said. "I understand it can be hard for a woman to go with a man standing nearby."

"Thank you," she said, glad he would find a female nurse. "Men are lucky to be able to go anywhere."

"We are," he said as he eased her back down. "Though it can also be hard for a man to pee while in bed. It's not the easiest thing to do."

He left the room and soon a female nurse came in his place.

"Destry said you're feeling ready to go," she said, coming up to Emma.

She'd never seen this nurse before.

This one didn't introduce herself. Instead, she picked up the bed pan and situated it near Emma. "Lift up, so I can scoot it under you," she said.

Emma lifted and held herself up with her arms though they shook, and her shoulder started hurting.

"It's common not to be able to go with a male nurse around. Female nurses are better."

But Emma still couldn't go.

After looking at the clock three times, showing her

impatience, the nurse said, "If you can't go, we'll put a catheter in."

Emma frowned. "I don't want one of those."

"Then go, or you have no choice," the nurse said, abrupt.

I can't relax enough with her, either. I want to get up.

Her frustrated thoughts were interrupted when Destry popped his head in around the door. "All good?"

"She won't go," the nurse said, as if it was something Emma willingly wouldn't do. "I've got to get back."

"Thanks," Destry said. Then the woman was gone.

Emma was glad she had Destry for a nurse and not the woman who'd never even given her name. She guessed that was one way to avoid complaints from patients.

Not that she'd complain about the impatient woman. She was just glad that she was gone.

Destry turned to her. "No luck?"

She shook her head.

"Let's try something." He went over to the sink in the room and turned it on so she could hear it running. "That might help," he said. "Ready to try again?"

"Yes," she said.

He'd said nothing about a catheter, which the other nurse seemed in a hurry for.

"I don't want to have to use a catheter," she said, before he could bring it up.

"Then let's get it done," he stated in a tone that told her he had no doubt she could do what needed doing.

He came back to her and helped her up over the pan again. "Listen to the water and think about peeing."

She did and it felt like she needed to go more than ever, but she was still having no luck.

"Put your hand on your lower belly, create more pressure. Sometimes that helps," he said.

She moved her hand down to her lower belly and pressed creating pressure on her bladder. "Oh my God, please go."

"Dear God, help her to pee," he said. "There, I'll pray with you."

Now we're both praying for me to ... the thought of asking God to help her pee brought up a giggle which burst out, and she laughed, the laughter making her relax enough and then it was like a waterfall had been turned on.

My God the relief. Oh, thank you.

She'd never known how bad it hurt to need to go and be unable to.

"Laughter works every time," Destry said. "All done?"

"Yes," she said. "Thank you."

Never thought I'd need to go in front of a man, she thought. *Especially a handsome one like Destry.*

If anyone had asked her if she could have, she would have told them it was impossible.

She hardly knew Destry. But he made her feel as if she could do anything. And he'd made an uncomfortable and embarrassing situation easier for her.

"You're welcome," he spoke if he'd done nothing special.

But for her, he really had.

"Be back in a minute," he said, as he took the bed pan into the bathroom.

She could see him through the open doorway, measuring the contents, before dumping them into the toilet.

She grabbed a wipe and cleaned herself then tossed it

into a nearby trashcan, making a basket before he came back out.

Yes. There was just something about making a basket. Succeeding. Two wins.

He came back out, put the bedpan in the corner out of the way, and then typed things into the computer.

She found herself watching every move he made, as he drew her gaze like a magnet.

"Why did you measure it?"

"To make sure everything is working," he said.

He came back over to check the bag of fluid hanging near her bed with the line connected to her right arm. "This one is nearly empty," he said. "I can take this line out now."

He removed the line and then wetted a washcloth and wiped her arm off before placing a Band-Aid on.

"Better?" he asked.

She nodded.

He gestured to her left arm. "We can do the other arm, where they gave you blood."

She glanced at her arm, wishing she could take a shower and clean everything. "I wish we could take all these things off of me," she said.

He bent over her, to look at her head where it felt itchy. "Has anyone offered you a sponge bath?"

"No," she said, and felt herself turning red as her cheeks heated at the same time.

Surely, he isn't going to sponge bathe me. Is he?

Conflicting feelings about the idea filled her.

Destry moved over to the sink and ran water into a small tub before dropping a washcloth into it, then he picked up the soap, and brought everything over to set on her bedside table.

He's so easy to watch. And to listen to.

He reached for the washcloth then wrung it out and handed it to her.

"You can wash your face first," he said. "Then I'll help with your hair."

"Okay," she said, relieved she'd keep her hospital gown on.

In the dream life of her imagination, she wanted him to bathe her. Every part of her. The thought was making her face heat again and the rest of her was catching up.

But she was much too shy for anything like that to happen.

Already Destry had taken her beyond where she'd gone with a boyfriend, to a more intimate level, as if it was no big deal.

To Emma it was a very big deal, but she couldn't let on to him.

He's being professional. Just doing his job.

I'm the one thinking inappropriate things.

She needed to stop.

After cleaning her face, she handed him the washcloth.

He dipped the cloth in the water and then wrung it out and leaned over her head.

With gentle swipes of the warm, wet washcloth, he began to clean the blood out of her hair and off the side of her scalp where it had dried.

The first swipe felt so good, warm and soothing, that she closed her eyes.

He's very good at this.

She couldn't help thinking of him washing other parts.

"I would have liked this to be cleaned up sooner," he said. "It can get busy in the ICU, and then things like this get put on a back burner."

Relaxing beneath his warm cleansing strokes and listening to his voice, she could have fallen asleep.

He can talk to me every night.

Sigh.

Talk me to sleep.

His voice was incomparable.

Too soon he was done, the blood had been cleaned away, and he stopped.

She'd kept her eyes closed so she heard him take the dirty water pan into the bathroom, dump it, and then flush.

As she watched him come back out, she said, "Why didn't you just pour it into the sink?"

"Too bloody," he said, in a British accent.

Though he was probably trying to make her laugh, the thought of blood on her head from the bullets that had hit her, and Mr. Smalls made her lose her sense of humor.

He handed her a towel to dry off with. "Better?" he asked.

"Yes," she said.

"I could ask one of the female nurses to give you a real sponge bath," he said. "But you'll be in a regular room soon and they may not get to it before they move you."

"I'll be in a regular room?"

"They won't keep you in ICU much longer, now that you're out of danger."

She couldn't tell him she was still in danger, with a cartel after her.

But she really wanted to. She wanted to tell him everything. There was a way about him that made her feel he was dependable and could be trusted.

But Mr. Smalls had said not to trust anyone.

So, she just said, "good."

"Once you're on a regular floor," he said. "You'll be able

to use the shower there. It will have a shower seat, so after your nurse walks you in, you'll be able to sit and take a shower by yourself."

"That sounds heavenly," she said. "A whole-body shower."

"Ready for something to drink?" he gave her a smile which made her feel all melty. "We've got apple juice and cranberry juice."

"Apple," she said.

"I'll be back with the juice and your meds," he said, taking the rolling thing that held the fluid bag with him.

Emma rubbed her right arm where the IV had been. Her arm felt better now, as did her head. She was thankful that Destry had partially cleaned her up.

When he returned with chilled apple juice and a straw, he put them on her bedside table and rolled it over to her across her lap. "We keep juice in the fridge on this floor, so if you want another, just ask."

"Okay, thank you," she said.

He handed her a little white paper cup with pills in it. "We're moving you off those soon." He gestured to the other lines in her arms. "Your meds will then all be in pill form. These will get you started. Let me know if you have trouble swallowing pills."

"It will be good to be off of them," she said. "I'm tired of being hooked to all this stuff. And no trouble taking pills."

"It is good," he said with a deep smile. "Progress."

He brought her the remote, and then showed her how to press the nurse's button on the side of her bed. Stuff she'd been too sleepy to need or want before. He also placed a small hospital phone on her table. "In case you have anyone you want to call," he said. "To let them know that you're all right."

She shook her head. "No one," she said, though she thought of her mother.

For a moment, she wished she could call her mother and father to let them know she was all right. The last time she'd spoken to her mother she'd just landed in Bozeman. Her family would worry when she disappeared.

They have no idea where I am. But neither does the cartel.

Destry watched her shake her head, but didn't say anything. Then he looked into her water pitcher. "Ice has melted," he said. "I'll get you some fresh ice."

Though she'd heard of male nurses, she'd never met one before Destry. She was amazed at how caring he was.

When he returned with fresh ice water and asked if there was anything else she needed, she said, "No. But I'm wondering about how you became a nurse. I've never met a male nurse before."

He nodded as if used to the question. "I enlisted in the Army, right out of high school, served and was trained as a medic. When I got out, I came home, got my RN degree, and got hired here at the Billings Clinic."

"So, you're from here," she said.

"Yes. Greybull, Wyoming, just a few hours away," he said. "I still have family there."

At this point, though she knew it was normal to then share something about herself in return, she just nodded.

Unable to share the truth about herself, she didn't want to make up lies for him. So, she didn't offer anything in return.

And anyway, she was tired of talking about herself and her medical. She would much rather listen to him and to learn more about him.

"What is Greybull like, Destry?"

"It's a small town," he said.

"Tell me about life there," she said. "Your family there."

"Mom and Dad, Gram, one uncle and his family of five, all live near Greybull The others are scattered about."

She'd grown quiet, so after he finished giving her meds and updating the forms on the computer, he stopped and turned to her, leaning on his rolling computer stand.

"Do you like dogs?" he asked.

"Yes, I love dogs," Emma said.

He smiled. "I've got a border collie named Scout."

"Oh, I like that name," she said with a smile. "Does he live up to his name?"

"Yes," Destry said. "He's a great herder, and he's the smartest dog I've ever had."

"Those are bigger dogs," she said. "We always had smaller dogs in my family. Grandma had a dash-hound."

"That is small," he laughed. "Border collies are considered mid-sized dogs. They're good working dogs. Good at herding cows and sheep."

"Oh, right," she said. "Do you have cows or sheep?"

"Just one horse, and one dog right now," he said. "But I'm planning to get a couple of cows soon."

"What's your horse's name?" she asked.

"Arrow," he said.

"Nice," she said. "Sounds a native American name."

"They would be more descriptive usually, like little arrow, straight arrow, etc."

"Well, I like Arrow," she said. "Both are great names."

"Where are you from?" he asked.

She'd made a mistake asking so much about him.

Naturally now he wanted to know about her. And she couldn't tell him. Not the truth anyway.

He watched her, patiently waiting for an answer.

"I'm from Indiana," she lied. She couldn't say Dayton, Ohio.

She'd only been to Indiana once, but both states were in the Midwest so her accent would match, if she had one.

She frowned.

What was the name of that town?

"Bloomington," she said at last, as it came to her.

Lying to him made her feel squeamish. She went quiet.

He waited again, watching her, and when she didn't say anything more, he said, "I'll leave you to your juice."

Though ordinarily she could have listened to him all day, she was ready for him to step out of the room, so she wouldn't have to lie again.

"Call if you need anything," he said.

She nodded and started sipping her juice.

* * *

Destry saw the way her gaze shifted away from him as she searched for an answer.

She appeared to be terrible at lying and was clearly unhappy about lying.

Though he hadn't known her long, he knew that much.

These weren't bad qualities to have, but why would she lie about where she was from? What was she running from?

He'd seen flickers of fear in her eyes when she was thinking and had let her guard down. Maybe it had been the meds helping her to let her guard down, but that quick flicker of truth was a glimpse into her real world.

She was a mystery he wanted to figure out. If he knew what she was afraid of, he would be better able to protect her and help her to lose that fear.

Had they met under other circumstances, he wouldn't have hesitated to ask her out.

* * *

She began flipping through TV channels trying to find an evening show to watch. Hoping to find a movie.

After drinking half her juice, she was thirsty and just wanted water. The pitcher was now sitting over near the sink in her room, so she sat up to ease out of the bed and go get some.

As she stood, a wave of dizziness hit her, and she swayed.

Destry chose that minute to walk into the room. Alarm on his face, he hurried to her side and helped her sit on the bed.

Her hands grasped the side of the bed and held on, as she waited for her dizziness to fade.

Destry crossed his arms across his chest which made her notice his muscles.

"What did you think you were doing?" He said, his gaze intent, as he watched her.

"I was just going to fill up my water pitcher," she said. "I'm thirsty."

"And you forgot to press the call button I showed you?" He raised an eyebrow, not pleased. "Whatever you need, I'll get for you. You need to rest. And see that board?" he pointed. "Where it says danger of falls? Till that goes away, don't try getting out of bed without me or another nurse."

"Okay," she said, her voice low. "I don't understand why I got dizzy. I was fine before."

"You've had surgery. You lost a lot of blood. You've been on strong medication. And you need to eat something. Any of those four things could make you dizzy, and you've had all four. Now let's get you back in bed and then I'll get you that water."

He swung her legs up onto the bed and under the covers as if they weighed nothing. And just like that, she was back in the hospital bed again.

She laid back on the pillows but watched him as he went to get her water.

To change the subject she said, "So, Destry. You're like one of those cowboys in the movies who ride and shoot people."

"I ride, sure." Destry shrugged. He brought the water pitcher to her. "But I haven't shot anybody stateside. I prefer to be more of a healer than a killer these days. Did enough of that on active duty."

"Oh, that's good," she said with a sigh. She'd been around enough shooting and had no desire to be around any kind of shooting again.

She was glad he was working as a nurse and not an active-duty soldier. Destry the RN she could dream about. Destry the soldier, not so much.

Soldiers often didn't come home. It would be a hard life being married to a soldier.

But she had to admit, if she'd met him as an active-duty soldier, it would have been hard to avoid being attracted to him.

It was hard enough here in the hospital where he was only taking care of her because of his job.

She was pretty sure that nurses and their patients were not supposed to be dating.

Though darn if her imagination wasn't working over-time again, making her imagine being together with him.

Ignoring everything which told her that she couldn't be with him.

She closed her eyes, knowing he might show up in her dreams.

* * *

Emma had slept through the rest of Destry's shift and didn't see him now.

His name was no longer on the white board, but no one had written a new name yet.

Her nurse Hannah came in. "Are you hungry?" she asked.

"I guess so," Emma said.

"What would you like? You're on a liquid diet to start with. We have orange or strawberry Jello, and chicken or beef broth, and more juice if you want that."

None of those sounded good.

"I guess chicken," she said. "Can you tell me when they'll move me?"

She wanted answers, not soup, now that she was more awake.

"We can let you know, once the orders are put in." The redhead wrote a name on the whiteboard. "I'm Terri, your night nurse."

She gestured to a dark-haired woman. "This is Hannah. Your day nurse. It's our shift change, so you'll see her again tomorrow morning, if you're still on this floor."

Emma, just blinked, and tried to be more awake.

She'd never been an early morning person, and usually woke slow.

"What happened to Destry?"

"He's switching over to another floor," Hannah said.

Another floor.

Sudden sadness that she wouldn't see Destry again overwhelmed her.

She didn't know why she was feeling so emotional about a man she'd just met. It made no sense.

"Glad you're awake now," Hannah said. "Good night!" She waved at her with a smile.

Emma waved back, then Hannah was out the door, and Emma let her hand drop.

"Still tired?" Terri asked.

"I guess," Emma said with a shrug. But that made her shoulder hurt and she winced.

"Are you in pain?" Terri asked.

"Yes," Emma said. "My shoulder hurts."

"It's going to," Terri said. "You're not due for pain meds for another hour."

It seemed like they were letting it go longer and longer before they gave her anything. Or maybe she was noticing it more now that she was awake more. Either way, it hurt.

"We can remove the heart monitor now though," Terri said. "I'm sure it will feel better to get those sticky pads off."

"Yes, please," Emma said.

Terri removed the pads and wires which monitored Emma's heart and then she removed the other IVs.

Emma's chest was sticky where the pads had been. She really wished she could have a shower now.

"Thank you," she said.

Terri brought her a menu and laid it on the table. "Once you're off the liquid diet, you can order from here. When you're ready, you can call in your meals on the phone," she said, and tapped the top of the paper. "Instructions are here, and it lists carbs and sugars, but if you can't figure it out, just ask them when you call. They'll add up what you can order."

"Okay." Emma picked up the menu and looked through it.

There wasn't anything on it to get excited about.

Her stomach growled.

How many hours has it been since I last ate real food?

She glanced at the closed door.

Terri had already left and there was no one to ask.

As busy as the nurses were, she wasn't going to press the call button just to ask a question.

Emma reached for the TV remote to try to find something to take her mind off everything. Flipping through channels, she found an old Doris Day movie she'd never seen and laid back on her pillow with a sigh.

I wonder how many hours I've been in here. And how soon I'll get out.

She wanted out of the hospital.

But where can I go after I'm out? I have no I.D., no bank cards, and very little cash.

Chapter Five

Destry couldn't get his new patient, Pearl Hayes, off of his mind.

His thoughts were on her as he ended his shift at the hospital.

She was special, and so was her situation.

Not that they weren't all special, at least to Destry, as he did his best to take care of each one.

Their needs varied, according to their illness.

But this young woman *was* special, because she'd been shot by four crazy gunmen from a Mexican cartel on the highway while heading to Billings and lived to talk about it.

She was lucky to be alive.

Her companion wasn't so lucky. He probably wasn't going to make it.

Destry knew what it was to have been shot at, and to shoot to win. He'd served in the Army in the special Ops team known as the Delta Force, one of the most silent and deadly teams the U.S. military deployed, to take down dangerous men and prevent bad things from happening.

He understood the trauma Pearl Hays had been through.

The men who shot her, and he companion, were dead, and connected to a Mexican cartel, the Sinaloa.

This had happened in Montana, which was crazy. Not at all like most Americans expected Montana to be.

That it had happened near where he'd been born and raised, with no cartels being active in the area when he was growing up, made it seem all the crazier to Destry.

He'd fought in South and Central America, and expected this kind of crime there, but not in Montana.

Destry had heard cartels had been moving into Montana, and with the spread of drugs in the area recently, he believed it.

Prior to this, there hadn't been this kind of crime in Montana, or Wyoming, where almost all locals carried a gun, and would put a stop to anyone trying to shoot anyone else dead. Where neighbors had looked after neighbors and there were no school shootings likely because most of the teachers carried.

That was the Montana he had grown up in.

Criminals looked for a soft target and it was harder to find them in Montana.

At least it had been that way when he was young.

Destry had always believed you had to be a special kind of stupid to pull a gun on anyone around here. Odds were, you'd be the one who would end up dead.

Which was exactly what had happened to the four cartel men who had opened fire on a young woman traveling in Montana. Though it was the local sheriff, two deputies, and a few other members of a DEA task force who'd ended their lives, and their killing spree, not a friendly bystander.

This month he he'd been working with patients who'd just made it into ICU.

Like his new patient, Pearl.

She'd awakened finally, but then gone back to sleep, which could be the meds, or it could be a way of escaping the dangers of her waking world. The temptation might be to want to keep taking things to stay asleep as a way of escaping the reality of dealing with the aftermath of her ordeal.

Part of his job was to wean her off certain pain meds, and help her be fully awake, fully functioning and healing.

He also hoped he could help her ease her mind and her body as she mended.

Apparently, others at the hospital had the same idea, as he was being shifted from ICU to a regular floor where they'd soon be moving her.

The next time he saw her, she would be on a regular floor.

Few people knew where she'd be next, or that he'd specifically been assigned as her nurse, which he realized was a security issue.

Her security was a major issue.

It was no small thing to be shot at, especially for a civilian female. But to have the cartel after her had to have been terrifying. Likely it still was.

He'd noticed she told him little about herself. And what she had said was likely a lie.

She claimed she didn't have anyone she wanted to call.

That was likely a lie. She'd thought of someone.

He'd seen it on her face and in her eyes. He'd also seen fear in those pretty green eyes.

Fear he'd like to clear away.

The day nurse said Pearl had slept restlessly now that the pain meds were wearing off.

He knew she'd been having nightmares.

As he drove past a fence line on his way home, where two horses stood by the fence, the sight briefly reminded him he needed to call his uncle.

Uncle Frank had called him on the way in to work and invited him to do some team roping this week and to talk about the rodeo roping team.

In his spare time, Destry didn't mind helping his dad, or his uncle and cousins with team roping, if they needed a hand on the ranch, or at the rodeo.

But he couldn't commit to the rodeo circuit right now, so that would be a no.

And this was the main reason he didn't.

He thought of how Pearl had appeared in the hospital bed the first time he'd seen her as she slept.

Her dark blonde hair, spread across her pillow, had given her an angelic look.

She was beautiful, he'd thought. *And too young to be in the ICU hooked to machines. Nearly dying. She'd lost a lot of blood, had been dehydrated, with blood sugar so low she couldn't have eaten recently.*

It was his job to help her recover, so she could walk out of the hospital.

From ICU to walking out the door. That was the kind of trophy he was after these days. Seeing his patients improve and go back to their lives, that was the best kind of trophy.

You couldn't wear it on a shiny new silver belt buckle, and no one was going to give you a medal for it, but you could wear it in your heart and mind, and know you'd helped someone.

It gave him great satisfaction.

He'd met the police guard outside the door before he entered his patient's room.

Because the cartel had tried to kill her, an officer would always be posted outside her door.

This was the first situation like this that Destry had encountered.

He'd immediately gone into a mode he'd sometimes used after getting out of the Army, where he'd had to be continually situationally aware.

That hyper awareness was now in full force.

He would notice anything, or anyone, out of place, and he had the skills to stop them, if someone got past the police officer on guard.

These days he preferred saving lives, but if saving a patient's life meant stepping up, to stop a bad guy, he had no problem doing that.

It just wasn't what he'd expected here, in Billings, Montana, when he'd come home.

He'd lived a quiet life since returning, and when working inside the hospital, he didn't carry a gun. He kept it locked in his truck.

But from now on, he'd better be prepared for anything.

* * *

Emma was awake and had just finished eating, when the sheriff came in to see her.

He stepped through the door wearing his uniform, and at the sight of him she startled just a little, her eyes widening.

I must remember to be Pearl now, not Emma. I can't tell him who I really am.

"Miss Pearl, I'm Sheriff Colt," Sheriff Colt said as he came into her room. "Brett Colt." He approached her bed. "I'm glad to see you're awake and doing better."

She nodded. "Thank you, Sheriff Colt, and to your men, for saving my life," she said.

"Glad we could be there in time," he said. "You got lucky. Now, we need to talk about what happened." He laid a folder on her bedside table and pulled it in front of her, but didn't open it.

"I have some pictures here that I need you to look at. They may be hard for you to look at, but I need you to try to identify these men."

He opened the folder and picked up the first picture, holding it in front of her so she could see it clearly.

She looked at a photo of a Hispanic looking man, dead on the highway and frowned at the sight of the dead body.

His neck and face were covered in tattoos and his clothes were dark. Bullet wounds had left a bloody mess.

Though not normally squeamish, seeing this man made her stomach start acting up and she wished she hadn't had those scrambled eggs which hadn't been all that good.

She'd wondered when she ate them how anyone could screw up scrambled eggs.

"I've never seen him before," she said. "I hadn't seen any of those men before they started shooting at us. So, I don't know who he is. They pulled up so fast next to us."

"He's a member of a Mexican cartel," the sheriff said. "The Sinaloa cartel. Have you heard of them?"

She shook her head. "No."

"These are some real bad guys. Involved in smuggling drugs, guns, and women."

She wrinkled her forehead. It was a world she knew nothing about.

"I don't know anything about any Mexican cartel."

He watched her chipping at the pink nail polish on her left thumb with her other thumb.

She hadn't realized she was doing that again. The nervous habit emerged when she was under stress.

Now it had caught his attention.

She stopped.

He pulled the second photo out to show her the next man.

This one, also Hispanic, had long hair, and a facial scar.

"No, I haven't seen that one either," she said with a shake of her head.

When he pulled out the third photo, this one had half of his head shaved and tattoos on his head as well as his neck.

She grimaced at the sight of him.

"No, I don't know him," she said. "Why do those men have tattoos all over their necks and heads?"

"Often those type of tattoos are obtained in prison," he said. "Some of the tattoos are gang markings."

"I wouldn't have thought they could go to tattoo parlors while in prison," she said. "They don't get out for that do they? And tattoos are expensive."

"They don't get out," he said. "They give each other homemade tattoos with things they smuggle in or make in there. Many things can be used to make a tattoo."

"I would have remembered if I'd seen any of those men. They're so scary looking with tattoos all over them. Sorry I'm not more help, but I haven't seen them anywhere."

"There's one more," he said. "This last one will be harder to look at. But we need you to figure out why they came after you and Mr. Smalls. If they'd been watching you, one of them might have been in a grocery store or a gas station watching."

"Okay," she said.

He placed the fourth photo in front of her.

This guy was clean cut, with shaved hair, unlike the others and had no tattoos. But he was harder to look at because he'd been shot in the head and was missing half of his face.

"Eww," she said, looking away, suddenly feeling queasy, her breakfast talking to her. She pulled her right hand up to cover her mouth.

"Take a moment to catch your breath," the sheriff said.

When she'd taken a few deep breaths and was feeling better she looked back at him.

"Better?" he asked.

"Yes," she said. "Better."

"Good," he said. "Now. Do you know the fourth man?"

"No."

"Sorry to have to put you through that," he said and glanced over at Destry who'd hurried in to check on Emma.

"Are you upsetting my patient, Sheriff Colt?" Destry said.

"Only briefly, as a necessity," he said. "I'm done now."

Destry came to her bedside and checked her blood pressure, which was up. "We'll wait a few minutes and then check it again," he said.

"My stomach is upset," she said. "I shouldn't have had those eggs for breakfast."

"I can give you something for it, if it's bad, but how about trying a few crackers? We keep some on the floor in case a patient needs them."

"Okay, I can try one or two," she said.

Reassured that Emma was all right, he turned to the sheriff. "No more today, because she needs her rest, agreed?"

The sheriff nodded. "Agreed."

He looked back to Emma. "One last thing before I go. Do you have any family or friends for us to notify that you're in the hospital, to let them know you're going to be okay?"

Emma's stomach rebelled even more. She didn't like lying to this nice man who'd saved her life, but Mr. Smalls had said, 'Trust no one.' And she supposed that meant even the sheriff.

"No," she said, her mind racing.

She didn't have a job to go back to, as her boss was dead.

"No one is expecting me to go back to work after this vacation," she said. "I don't have a job anymore. So, I don't have to call in."

At least that part isn't a lie.

He watched her closely. "Sorry to hear that. What about relatives?"

"I don't have any relatives still living," she said as she felt her face flushing. "Or friends that I'm close to, so no. There's no one."

"That's too bad," he said. "Well, if you think of anyone, let me know, and I'll get in touch with them."

"Okay," she said. Though there was no way she would be able to do that. It wasn't safe.

My family can't know I'm here. Neither can any of my friends.

None of them are going to know what happened to me.

Those thoughts made her sadder than she'd ever been in her life. And she couldn't talk to anyone about it.

Hannah came in after the sheriff left. "I have good news," she said. "You're moving to a regular floor tomorrow, after the doctor makes rounds and checks on your wound."

Emma said, "That's great. Maybe I'll be able to take a shower then."

"I'm sure you will," Hannah said.

"Where's Destry?" Emma asked.

It wasn't time for a shift change yet.

"He's in a meeting right now, so I'm filling in," Hannah said. "When he's done, he's headed home so you won't see him again tonight."

"Okay," Emma said, but she couldn't help feeling sad. She liked it when Destry was here and missed him when he was gone.

Perhaps Hannah read disappointment on her face because before she left the room, she said, "If you want a midnight snack tonight, we have vanilla ice cream or chocolate pudding to choose from. Just let us know."

Funny, Destry hadn't offered me any vanilla ice-cream or chocolate pudding. If he were here, I'd ask him what was up with that.

Would he be home tonight, throwing a frisbee for his dog, Scout and would he ride his horse, Arrow?

She would love to see that. The next time she saw him she would ask to see pictures of them.

* * *

The next day, after Pearl had been moved to a regular floor, the sheriff had come to see her again, to see if she remembered anything else about the men that had shot her. He'd asked her about family and friends and she'd had to tell him again, she had no one.

Once the sheriff left her room, Destry asked him to step to the side so they could talk, before Emma knew Destry was there. He was looking forward to surprising her.

"What can you tell me about these cartel guys?" Destry said.

"This wasn't a problem when I was growing up over in Greybull. Things have changed since I enlisted."

"Which branch were you in?" the sheriff asked.

"Army," Destry said.

"And what did you do in the Army, Mr. Walsh?"

Destry answered in a low voice. "Special Ops. Delta Force."

"Well, I suppose you'll have a security clearance, which should check out," Sheriff Colt cleared his throat.

"It will," Destry said.

The sheriff continued. "We have specific intelligence that primarily two drug cartels based out of Mexico are operating here in Montana on a very large scale. The Sinaloa cartel is one and the men that were killed were Sinaloa."

"Thank you," Destry said. "I'll stay on alert for trouble. You have a man on the door, so that makes two. But it may not be enough to keep her safe."

"Normally we would just keep one man near your patient, and he'd keep an eye on her, as well as anyone that went in or out and she'd be fine under police protection. But I agree, this situation is different, and you are correct. One man guarding her may not be enough."

"I have certain skills, Sheriff," Destry said. "Far beyond police training."

"I understand you're ex-military and have that training," the sheriff said. "But you don't know these people. The people after her, they are ruthless. And she needs to disappear. Here in the hospital, she's a sitting duck. We need to get her to a safer place, once the doctor says she's good to go."

"And have you talked to the doctor?" Destry said. "What does he say about all this?"

"He would prefer the cartel not send men in here, to shoot the place up and try to kill her. And the people we're talking about would have no qualms about doing just that."

"The cartels won't get away with as much here in Montana," Destry said. "Most everyone carries."

"Though not likely they'll be carrying in the hospital," the sheriff said.

"True." Destry nodded, thinking about his nine-millimeter. He didn't mention it.

"The cartels are here in Montana, and it's a problem." The sheriff shook his head. "Just ask anyone with the highway patrol. The cartel comes through here, and every time they bring another semi, loaded with young women they're trafficking, drugs or guns. Patrolmen are having trouble, because if they pull them over, without proper back up, they're likely to be shot."

He paused. "There can be many cartel men here, for an operation like shutting this young woman down, for good. And when they come in heavy, they often leave a scorched earth behind them."

Destry's jaw dropped, hearing this, as it was much worse than he'd expected, but he pulled himself together quick. "What do you need me to do?" he asked.

"For now, I'm asking you to guard the woman, and to see to her nursing. Think you can do both?"

"I'll be focused on her when nursing. But I can also keep an eye out for anyone out of place. I already do that. It's become second nature."

"I'd like two men on her protection detail," Sheriff Colt sad. "A man's got to sleep sometime. But we're shorthanded, which is why I'm asking for your help."

"That he does," Destry agreed. "I'm happy to help. Do you have any what has she's done to make the cartel want to come after her?"

"Not yet, but we're working on that," sheriff Colt said. "There's got to be a reason."

* * *

The morning had been slow to start as she waited for the doctor to make his rounds and check on her wound.

He'd okayed her to be moved to a regular room, so after he'd seen her, the nurses put her things in a plastic bag and set it on the end of her bed.

The guy who came to move her brought a different kind of bed and was apparently going to roll her down the hall in it.

"Can't I walk?" she asked.

"Not this time, Hun," her nurse said. "But it won't be long until you're walking out of here."

"Okay," Emma said, and tolerated them moving her from one bed to the other.

Her nurses told her goodbye, and then she was being rolled down the hall, which gave her a weird feeling, kind of nauseating.

So, she closed her eyes and stayed still.

Guess I'm still tired. And the lights overhead are bright.

Riding with eyes closed, she didn't see the man standing guard outside her new room. Then she was inside resting in her new room.

I hope my nurses here are nice, more like Destry and less like that nameless woman.

The move had worn her out, but it wasn't long until the sheriff was visiting her again, so she didn't really sleep.

Again, he had questions she either could not or would not answer. But at least she didn't have to repeat lies. She just told him she hadn't remembered anything more.

After he'd been gone about twenty minutes, the door to her room opened and she looked over to see Destry entering.

"Destry!" she cried with surprise. "Did you come to visit?"

"Hello Pearl," he said with a smile.

She wished it was her real name he was saying, though she liked the way her middle name sounded on his lips.

"I came to take care of you," he said. "I've been assigned to this floor."

"You have?" her eyes widened, unable to believe her good luck. Then she smiled back at him. "I'm glad."

"Me too," he said. "How are you feeling today?"

"Better now that I've seen you," she said.

The words were out before she could stop them. They were her honest feelings, but still...

She blushed.

"It's good to see you too," he said. "Do you need anything before I get your meds?"

"Not a thing," she said.

Having him here really made her day. More than anything she would have asked for.

"But I do have one complaint," she said.

"What's that?" he asked.

"Why didn't you offer me any vanilla ice-cream or chocolate pudding the other night?" she asked. "I had both last night."

"Both?" He laughed. "Sorry darlin,' I forgot to offer any. But it sure sounds like you made up for that." He winked.

If she could have swooned through her bed down to the

floor, she would have at the sight of him winking at her and that tease in his voice.

"Oh, I did," she said. "Well, if you forget again tonight, I'll need to have both."

"You will?"

"Yes, sir, I certainly will."

He got a strange look on his face when she said sir. Maybe because of his military service.

She'd known one other man who didn't like to be called sir, and one of her girlfriends from school had once had a boyfriend who'd insisted on it.

"No need to call me sir," he said.

"Just Destry will do."

"All right, Destry," she said.

Destry nodded, and said, "I'll go get your meds."

Emma nodded back.

She loved listening to his voice and was happy to be able to listen to him again.

After her meds kicked in and she'd rested more than she wanted to after eating another meal, Destry came into the room, with purpose. It got her attention.

"Let's get you up and walking," he said.

"Okay," she said, glad somebody wanted her up and back to her old life.

Though God knew she couldn't go back to her former life right now. And who knew when she could.

He helped her walk slowly to the bathroom, and once she was inside, he closed the door to give her privacy.

This is like a 180 from him helping me to use a bed pan.

The privacy once she was situated inside was something she'd missed.

Though a little dizzy, she was on the mend and feeling much more normal. She eyed the shower and wondered how soon she'd be allowed to take a whole-body shower. It would make her feel better.

When she was done, she called for him and he helped her walk back and then get into bed.

She was surprised by how tired that short trek had left her. She'd never been in a hospital before, or had any kind of health issues, so many aspects of what she was experiencing were new.

She was glad none would be permanent. If she had her way, she'd never be in a hospital again.

Tired, she fell asleep.

In her dream, the men were back. They were coming for her. The van was chasing her, and the door was opening.

She turned her head and tried to run.

Destry entered her room to check on her.

She'd tossed her sheet and blanket off and was moving about as she slept, clearly having a bad dream.

He went over to her without touching her, for he knew better than to do that. "Pearl," he said. "Wake up."

Still, she rolled, kicking out with her legs, the nightmare not letting her go.

"Pearl!" he said her name louder and she stopped.

Her eyelids flashed open, those green eyes staring at him, her breathing ragged.

"You were having a bad dream," he said, softer now that he'd awakened her.

"You're in the Billings Clinic," he told her, to help her orient herself. "In your room. Safe."

"They were back," she said. "They were trying to kill me."

"It was a dream," he said. "Those men are dead. They can't come back. But I know how a dream can seem real."

"It's like I live it over and over when I sleep," she said.

""I understand," he said.

"It makes me not want to sleep. I'll see that van pull up and then the door opens and they are there again, shooting at me."

"You might have dreams like that for a while," he said. "It could be good to talk to someone."

"I don't want a shrink," she said. "I'm not crazy."

"Of course you're not," he said. "But you've been in a gun battle, and that can affect the toughest warriors. Sometimes it helps to talk it out."

"I'll think about it," she said.

Right now, she just wanted to sleep.

"It's so cold in this room," she said.

"Losing your blanket didn't help," he said.

She noticed he didn't say kicking off her blanket, which she'd done while dreaming.

She'd also kicked off one hospital sock and the other was half off her foot, dangling. No wonder her feet were cold.

As he went to fix both her socks, he said, "Your feet are like ice cubes. Would you like a warm blanket?"

That sounded so good. "Yes please."

Destry made sure she was comfortable and warm enough beneath the sheet, and a fresh warm blanket, as he tucked her back in.

She smiled up at him.

He was the best.

Once her toes were warm, it wasn't long until she fell back to sleep.

She slept without dreaming of bad men, but instead dreamed of Destry. The opposite of a bad dream, it was better than her daydreams.

* * *

As he came in the room to check on her, she had awakened from a much nicer dream. One in which he was showing her his ranch, while they rode on horses. Now she wanted to know more about his animals.

"Do you have pictures of your animals?"

"Yep. Sure do," he said. "I'll show them to you tonight before I go home."

"I can't wait to see them," Emma said.

She loved dogs and though she'd never been around horses, she loved all animals, except for snakes. Snakes terrified her. She couldn't even watch them on the TV.

Chapter Six

Destry was worried about Pearl.

The police had an officer making sure only medical personnel went into her room. He hoped that was enough.

The cartel operating in the western states was one of the worst out of Mexico.

They slunk their way in like a poisonous snake, wriggling in beneath notice into the reservations, cozying up to the Indian women, and giving out drugs.

As a result, crime had gone up.

Falling under tribal law enforcement there wasn't much the local sheriffs or police officers could do about it.

At the hospital they were seeing more deaths from fentanyl, and more gunshot wounds than usual and it showed no signs of slowing down.

It would be easy for someone connected to the cartel to enter the hospital and find Pearl.

The Billings Clinic hadn't been made to keep people out, but to let them in to help them.

The handful of security guards that worked there wouldn't be enough to stop one or more determined men.

Ultimately it would be best to release Pearl so she could go to a safer location.

It was time to talk to Sheriff Colt. He asked the patrolman on duty if Sheriff Colt would be coming around soon and then asked if he would send a message to him, that Destry wanted to talk to him.

The patrol said he would pass the message along.

Destry thanked him and went to check on Pearl.

* * *

The sheriff arrived and stood waiting for Destry near the nurse's station when he came to leave a message for the doctor.

"Destry," the sheriff nodded at him.

"Glad you stopped by," Destry said.

"How's the patient?" Sheriff Colt asked.

"She's in good health and improving rapidly," Destry said. "What's the plan after she's released?"

"Haven't made one yet," Sheriff Colt said.

Destry had thought Pearl's situation over and come up with what he thought was the best solution for her.

"She can stay with me," he said. "She'd be hard to find at my place, if they even knew to look for her there."

"Where is your place?" Sheriff Colt asked him.

Destry told him and the sheriff nodded.

"I know that area."

"It's off the main road and most people don't even know the house is back there. In fact, people have trouble finding me the first time they come out."

"Yes, I can see how that would be, in that area," the sheriff said.

"I, or my neighbors, would notice anyone we don't know who comes up that road."

"Telling your neighbors would add more people to the list of who could be bribed." the sheriff's concerned gaze met Destry's.

"I don't plan on telling them," Destry said. "Just saying my neighbors, we look out for each other."

"Alright, we're agreed," Sheriff Colt said. "You and I will be the only ones who know where she is," he said. "So there will be no leaks."

"Good," Destry said.

The sheriff's radio went off and he answered it. "On my way," he said. As he put his radio away, he said, "The news needs to come from me. I'll tell her when I come back."

"Of course," Destry said.

That would be more appropriate than him telling her. He didn't want her to be nervous about staying at his place.

While she was staying with him, he would keep his eye on her, as well as seeing to any medical care she might still need.

His place between Billings, Montana and Cody, Wyoming had a large stretch of land, a small one-story ranch house, with a barn, one horse, and a dog. He lived alone far off the main road and would see anyone coming to his house long before they reached it. With no trees, there was no cover for sneaking up on him, just the way he liked it.

It would be the best place to hide Pearl. His three-bedroom ranch house had plenty of room. She could have one of the three bedrooms. The second one was always reserved for Gram.

When gram visited his place, sometimes she needed a nap, so the room was hers, and if she was ever too tired to make the drive home by herself at night, which had happened once or twice, she could stay over.

Gram might want to come out. He would cross that bridge when he came to it.

The last time she'd visited, he'd convinced her to take a nap in the guest bedroom and she'd snored for an hour. He grinned.

He didn't worry about telling gram about Pearl. She could keep a secret with the best of them and was very trust worthy. He wouldn't mention Pearl on the phone because lines could easily be tapped.

Nor was he going to mention gram to the sheriff.

Few could keep secrets as well as his family. And his family had a fierce history of defending family. When they closed ranks around you, it was the safest and warmest place to be. Because then you were family too.

* * *

Destry's cousin Jake Summers was a SEAL stationed in Virginia, when he wasn't deployed on a mission. Destry picked up the phone to call Jake, hoping his cousin would be in country and able to take a call.

"Hey, Destry, what's up, man?" his cousin sounded surprised to hear from him. "The fam out there all doing all right?"

"Yeah, we're all fine out here," Destry said. "You stateside for a while?"

"A few days at least," Jake said. "No problem but let me call you back in a few."

"Okay."

Destry had just enough time to let Scout out to do his business and to refill his water bowl when his cousin rang back.

"Hey, what've you got?" Jake asked.

"Special circumstances here now," Destry said.

"Which you can't say over the phone."

"Right."

"Any new fillies out your way?" Jake switched to the code talk of their childhood and was asking if a girl was involved.

"Saw one just last week," Destry said. "Should have a new one at my place soon."

"Good to hear. Hey, Destry, I've got to go. But keep in touch. And call me if you need me."

"Will do."

"Tell gram, I'll try to make it for the fourth."

He always tried to make it to the big family Fourth of July celebration and he'd made it two times out of six times since enlisting. Life as a Navy SEAL didn't stop for holidays, he had just been lucky those times.

"I will," Destry said. He knew she would ask if he'd heard from his cousin, and she'd be glad that they'd talked.

"Hey, you going to the fourth of July rodeo this year?"

Jake had grown up with Destry before Jake's mother, Mary Jayne Summers, a widow, remarried and moved his cousin to Oklahoma.

The boys had spent plenty of time riding in rodeos as they were growing up.

"You know it," he said.

Destry having two tickets to the 4th of July rodeo was always a given. "Want to join me?"

"Maybe," Jake said. "No promises though."

"Okay no worries," Destry said. "I know the drill."

Jake would never commit as he never knew if he'd be out of the country. But if he was able to, he'd hop on a plane and make it out to see the family.

Once they hung up, Destry threw the doggie frisbee for his Scout a few times and then called him to go in.

Destry's stomach was growling, and his dog needed to be fed.

He had six hours until he had to be at the hospital again.

His shift work was usually a rotation of twelve hours on followed by twelve hours off.

* * *

Sheriff Colt was the one that broke the news to Emma the next time he visited.

He came into the room and said, "How are you feeling? About ready to be out of here?"

"Yes," she said. "But I don't know where I'm going or even where my things are. In the ER they told me they had to cut my shirt off, so I have nothing to wear when I leave here."

"Your things have been safe in my office," he said.

Deputy Brown entered the room, carrying her brown leather suitcase, her backpack, and her purse. He set the suitcase in the corner of the room and her backpack and purse on a chair.

"Thank you," she said.

"You're welcome," Deputy Brown and Sheriff Colt both said at once.

"Anything else?" Deputy Brown asked the sheriff.

"Nothing here," he said.

"Glad you're doing better," Deputy Brown said. Then he tipped his hat to Emma and was out the door.

The sheriff waited a minute after he left to speak. Then he lowered his voice. "They're releasing you tomorrow. We're keeping that quiet for your safety."

"Thank you," Emma said.

He pointed to her purse. "Never did find your I.D. at the scene of the crash."

"Oh, that's because I didn't have it with me," she said.

He looked at her, waiting for more.

"I lost it." She gave a nervous laugh.

Here she was, lying to the sheriff agin. And he'd saved her life. She really wished she could have been honest with him. But then it would get out who she was and anyone looking for her could find her.

"I see," he said. "Might want to get a new one soon."

"Yes sir."

"Anything new that you've remembered?"

"No, nothing new." Emma caught herself chipping away at the fingernail polish on her left thumb with her other thumb and stopped.

He nodded and then went to the door and gestured to someone outside her room.

Destry followed him back into her room.

"When you leave here," the sheriff said, "you're going to need to lay low for a while, for your safety."

She wanted to ask how long a while but didn't.

"Okay," she said, wondering where she could go. She'd brought very little cash with her, just enough to shop a little, and eat out a few times. Tip a driver.

It's not like I can use a bank card right now.

"You know Destry as the nurse who's been taking care of you, but what you might not know, is that Destry was in the Army's special forces. I don't know of anyone more qualified to work as your bodyguard."

"Bodyguard?" she squeaked.

Wait. Destry is special forces? He's going to be my bodyguard?

"Remember, the cartel tried to kill you," Sheriff Colt said. "And they may still be after you."

How could I forget?

"We have a plan for you, with your permission, which is the best option for you right now," the sheriff said. "You can stay on Destry's ranch, and finish healing in a safe place with a good man to guard you."

Her jaw dropped open.

Was he for real? Destry, the nurse I've been daydreaming about is now a special Ops warrior and will be my bodyguard while I live on his ranch?

This felt unreal.

She wanted to pinch her arm to check if she was dreaming.

This was more than her daydreams of being with Destry coming true, because in her wildest dreams she would never have thought up this one.

Never would she have imagined she'd be going to Destry's ranch.

She'd closed her mouth and was thinking.

Destry watched silently, waiting for what she thought of the idea.

"Yes, okay," she told the sheriff, and then she turned to Destry. "I'll look forward to meeting Arrow and Scout soon, and thank you so much for offering me a safe place to stay."

Relief filled him that she'd said yes.

"You're welcome," he said. "Happy to help."

He was happy that she wanted to meet his animals and looked forward to showing her his place.

* * *

Emma sat on the bed looking through the plastic bag which held her belongings, where the nurses had put everything she'd come into the ER with.

They'd cut the shirt she'd worn on the plane off her and tossed it in the trash. They'd salvaged her bra, jeans, socks and tennis shoes but nothing had been washed.

Looking at them now, she saw blood stains on her jeans, white tennis shoes, and her white socks.

She would leave all that in the bag until she could wash them. Her bra wasn't stained but it needed to be washed so she left it in the bag. Good thing she had her suitcase now.

Destry came into the room. "How are you doing?" he asked.

"I need to go through my suitcase," she said. "To get clothes out to wear when I leave."

Destry lifted her leather suitcase from the corner of the room and carried it over to sit it on top of the foot of the hospital bed.

"Try to avoid bright colors and anything that pulls attention," he said. "We need to get you into the truck without you catching anyone's attention."

"All right," she said.

She opened the suitcase and sorted through it until she'd found underwear and socks, a navy-blue T-shirt, a pair of jeans, and her brown sandals.

The bag of dirty clothes she stuffed into the suitcase. Next, she went through her backpack and then her purse. Once she'd finished, she sat looking at the three bags. The familiar things inside were the only things she had with her of her old life.

No one packs to go on vacation thinking of things they might want if they never make it back to their home. They take vacation things, temporary things. Sunblock, swimsuits, paperbacks to read on the beach. They don't take going on the run kinds of things like photos or mementos that mean something.

* * *

Destry was coming to get her the end of his shift. He'd already taken her bags down to store in his truck until they were ready to leave.

She was ready to leave with him. As ready as she could be to walk back out in public again.

She'd chipped most of her nail polish off. What was left made her fingernails look blotchy.

In her suitcase she'd packed nail polish remover wipes, and could use those after they got to his ranch.

Though she'd thought she'd be staying by herself in Montana, she'd packed nail polish, eye makeup, and colored lip balm. She'd even packed a packet of lavender bath salts for a relaxing treat.

These things were about treating herself, not how she looked.

Emma was supposed to be staying alone somewhere.

Where had he been planning to send me?

She suddenly realized she'd never know where her boss had been sending her.

I suppose that doesn't matter now.

Would he have been surprised at what happened to me? Or did he know those bad guys were coming?

Likely she'd never know the answer to that, either.

Now she was going to Destry's home and needed to focus on her future, not on the past.

Suddenly she cared very much about how she would look as she was staying with Destry, and was glad she'd packed beauty products.

Her vacation had taken quite a turn from what she'd imagined she'd be doing.

From restful relaxation to nightmare almost dying and being shot, to what would be a real ranch with a real live, handsome cowboy who made her feel melty inside just listening to him.

She was excited, but also nervous. Because leaving here meant going back out there, where there were bad guys who might try to kill her.

Her stomach twisted in knots.

Destry appeared in the doorway. "Ready to go?"

"Yes," she nodded.

She was wearing a navy-blue T-shirt, a pair of jeans, and her brown sandals. As he'd instructed, nothing to draw attention to herself.

The pink T-shirt with a large hand painted yellow daisy on the front was a definite no, so it stayed in the suitcase. Most of her clothing was more cheerful than what she had on now. She was more a yellow daisy kind of person and right now what she was wearing made her feel rather drab.

"Brought you something," he said. He was holding it behind his back.

"You did?" Surprise filled her.

He didn't have to bring me anything. He's already doing so much for me.

He whipped his hand around and held out a cowboy hat.

An off-white cowboy hat with a light tan band that had pink beads on it.

"Oh, my goodness!" she said. "This hat is for me?"

"Yes ma'am," he said. "It will help you to blend in. Out here, cowboy hats are seen on the regular, and you can hide your face beneath it."

"Oh, I love it," she said, reaching for the hat.

He stood smiling at her as he watched her place it on her head.

She wished she had a mirror to see how it looked. She could only tell by how it felt. It fit just right, as if it was made for her.

"Looks good on you," Destry said.

"Thank you," she beamed up at him. Suddenly she didn't feel so drab.

"Come on then," he said. "Let's go."

He took her to the employee elevator and down to the back parking lot. He'd parked his truck near the door.

Soon they were inside, driving away.

The scenic and peaceful drive to his home was the opposite of her drive to Billings, most of which was a blur in her memory.

Today the beautiful blue sky was dotted by a few white clouds, and she saw a bird flying across an open expanse of pasture.

Once away from Billings, they only saw one other truck which passed them, causing her to hold her breath.

But once the other truck had driven past them and kept going, she exhaled again.

They turned onto a narrow dirt road off the highway which looked like nothing was around it except pasture.

"Your house is back here?" she asked.

"Yes, ma'am."

"I wouldn't have guessed anyone lives here. It looks like nothing is back here."

"That's the idea, darlin' and that's why this is the safest place for you to hide out for a while."

I'm out west, wearing a cowboy hat, riding with a handsome, sexy cowboy, in his truck to his ranch, where I will be hiding out. Yeah, I'm living in a country song or a western movie.

Her heart whispered, 'a western love story.'

After they drove up and over hills and across a cattle guard, which the truck rumbled over, jiggling them a bit, she saw his home.

Destry had a small ranch style house painted white, and behind it, she could see a red barn with white trim.

In a fenced area next to the barn, stood a brown horse with white feet. It turned and then she saw a white blaze on its face.

"Is that Arrow?" she asked.

"The one and only," he said. "I can't afford more than one horse right now. Just built that barn last summer after the house was done. Cattle will be next."

"Everything looks great," she said. "Did you build the house yourself?"

"With some help."

The horse was watching his truck drive up to the barn.

Destry parked and then came around to help her out.

Once she was down out of the truck, she walked over to see Arrow closer. She turned to look at Destry who was striding toward her, and momentarily forgot what she was going to say.

He walked with a confident stride, that of a man who knew the land well, as if he were a part of the landscape, with that oneness and familiarity with the land. His long-legged stride, slow and deliberate, was all cowboy, more life-like than one from an old west movie.

Her cowboy had stepped right out of her dreams into her life and now suddenly she was standing on his ranch with him striding toward her.

He was incredibly sexy. She could watch him walk toward her all day. And if he spoke, in that voice, she was a goner.

The horse nickered and finally, her words came back to her, waking her from her walking daydream.

"He's real pretty," she said, as she gestured to his horse, her words now nervously tumbling out. "I don't know much about horses. Never ridden a horse before."

"Would you like to ride?" he asked, as he stepped close to her. "Darlin' if you want to ride a horse, I can certainly make that happen for you."

His voice and his nearness made her feel all melty inside.

Chapter Seven

Emma laughed nervously.

"Well, not now."

Destry grinned at her. "I didn't mean we'd go riding right this minute. Later, when you're ready to try going for a ride."

She felt her face heating and knew she was blushing.

"You're turning as pink as the decorations on your hat."

"I am?" she touched her fingers to her warm cheek and knew he was right.

"Yes, you are," he said. "Well, you just let me know when you want to go for a ride, and I will make that happen."

"Okay."

He moved closer to Arrow and put a hand on his neck. "Hey, boy, I brought a lady here for you to meet. This here is Pearl."

Turning to look at Pearl he said, "You can pet him. Go ahead."

She reached her hand out slow, tentatively touching his horses face. "Hello Arrow."

The horse nickered softly.

"It's like he said hello," she said.

"Yep," he nodded. He waited a few minutes watching her pet his horse and took in the joy on her face before he said, "Ready to meet Scout?"

"Oh, yes, where is he?"

"In the house. He was sleeping when I left. He'll be up now and needing to go out."

"Then what are we waiting for?" she asked.

He walked with her to the back door of his house.

They could hear the soft woofing of his border collie before he unlocked the door.

The moment he opened it, Scout was out the door, tail wagging, clearly needing to go out, but so happy to see him and to meet her, he had to do that before going to do his business.

The black and white dog appeared highly energetic.

"Scout, go pee," Destry said.

Giving one woof, Scout ran off to do just that.

"Come on in," Destry said, holding the door open for her. "He'll be back, after he marks his territory and then patrols around for a bit."

"Is he a good guard dog?" She asked.

"Yep. And a good herder which will be great, once I have a herd for herding. Right now, he only has Arrow and me, to herd."

She laughed.

"You laugh, but just wait. He'll be herding you too," Destry said. "Then you'll see what I mean."

"Looking forward to it," Emma said.

She followed him into the house and was immediately impressed by how clean it was. She'd seen both her brother's bachelor pads before they settled down and looking around Destry's place at first glance, it didn't resemble a bachelor pad. Someone kept this place clean.

There was a cozy kitchen with a western style table and chairs off to the side, and beyond it, a living room with a large stone fireplace. On the mantel were all manner of awards and above it, a painting of a cowboy on a bucking bronc.

As she stepped closer, and noted the familiarity of the cowboy's face, she turned to Destry with surprise. "That's you!"

"Yep," he said. "My aunt paints. She gave that one to me the Christmas after I enlisted, but I never had anywhere to hang it, so it stayed at grams house for a long while."

"It's a great likeness of you," she said, "And there's so much action in the painting."

"Darlin' that's nothing compared to the action on the back of a bronc or a bull."

"I've never been to a rodeo," she said.

"Never? Well, we can fix that, too. There's a rodeo in Cody, every night in the summer."

"Every night? Wow."

"Yep." He nodded. "Okay, come on and I'll show you to your room. You can start getting settled in."

"My bags are still in the truck," she said.

"I'll bring them in next," he said.

The guest room which would be hers was decorated with a queen-sized bed covered by a yellow, white and green quilt, in a wildflower pattern.

"Gram made the quilt," he said.

"It's beautiful," she said. "And cheerful."

"It is," he agreed.

On the wall was a painting of daisies in a field. She walked closer to look at it and saw his aunt's signature.

"Yep, my aunt painted that one," he said.

"You have some talented women in your family," she said.

"Yes, I do." He nodded. "Okay, the bathroom is across the hall, the bedroom next to it is grams and mine is at the end of the hall. You can look around while I bring your bags in."

The first thing she did was check out the bathroom. Decorated in a soft green, the room was so clean it hardly looked used. Maybe he didn't get many visitors.

His grams room was almost like hers except for the pale pink quilt with roses as a pattern, and a painting of a guardian angel looking over a woman sleeping in her bed. On a closer look, that woman was likely his gran.

What a loving gift to have painted for her mother. A nightly reminder she would see before she slept that her guardian angel is always there, looking over her.

It was a reminder for Emma as well. One she deeply needed.

Emma hurried on to Destry's room for a quick peek.

She really didn't want to be in there when he returned, though she'd been given permission. This was his private space.

Destry's room was all male. From western wooden furniture made from large logs to the red, white and blue star quilt on the bed and the blue pillows and curtains to match. Instead of a painting on the wall he had a native American dream catcher and a photo of an eagle soaring. He had a private bath attached to the room.

She was glad they wouldn't have to share a bathroom and looked forward to having the guest bath all to herself.

Hurrying back out of his room, she was just in time before he came through the door with her bags. He headed into her room and said, "Tell me where you want them."

"On the bed is good," she said.

"Feel free to use the closet and dresser. They're empty."

"Thank you."

Once he left her to it, she started unpacking. She found the three paperbacks she'd brought.

One mystery, one SEAL romance, and one cowboy romance.

Not sure which one she wanted to read first, she stacked all three on the bedside table.

Lately she was very much in the mood to read a cowboy romance, if her imagination was any indication of which she should start with.

She had a romance story going in her head already, but it featured a real live cowboy.

One who filled her dreams at night.

Emma went back to her unpacking until the two bags were empty and then set the suitcase and her backpack on the floor of the closet.

All done, she wasn't sure what to do with herself next.

She went into the living room to explore it and see what his trophies were for. She'd been too distracted by the painting of Destry to pay more attention to his trophies.

The trophies intrigued her. Everything about Destry intrigued her.

As she wandered about the room, touching trophies and memorabilia, reading their labels, Destry came into the room.

"You have so many trophies," she said. "Some of them from when you were young. How long have you been a cowboy?"

He grinned. "Out here, we start young. Around three or

four. As soon as we can ride a sheep, holding on, we can ride in the mutton busting competition at the local rodeo."

"Wow!" Her eyes widened. "That is young!"

"Our high schools have rodeo teams, just like your high school had football."

"That's cool," she said. "Do you still have high school football teams?"

"Of course," he laughed. "Nobody is getting rid of them."

"You grew up surrounded by rodeo," she said.

"Yep. We have many rodeo families out here. Did you know that Cody is known as the rodeo capitol of the world?"

She shook her head. "I had no idea."

"Buffalo Bill Cody founded the town, and his Wild West shows were so popular he even took them overseas. He performed for Queen Victoria in England."

"That's amazing," she said.

"She gave him a huge carved wooden bar which is still in the Erma hotel. Solid cherry."

"Oh, I would love to see that."

"I wish I could take you around and show you everything you wanted to see, but you need to stay out of sight, for now."

"I know," she sighed. "It sucks."

"It does," he agreed. "But you've got the run of my ranch. Explore as much as you want. We're remote enough you should be safer here, than any safe house they'd put you in, near people."

"I want to hear all about your rodeo days," she said. "Teach me about rodeo."

"I can do that," he paused and then said, "I can also show it to you. I've got two tickets to the rodeo, over fourth of July weekend and those tickets sell out every year, almost as soon as they offer them. I always get two tickets. So, if you'd like to go with me, I'd love to take you. It will be a large crowd, easier to blend in."

Her shining eyes looking up at him told him that asking her was a good idea.

"Yes!" She quickly answered. "I'd love to go."

"Then it's a date," he said.

He didn't know why he'd said that. But he had.

"I'll fire up the grill and fix some burgers," he said, changing the subject. "And if you don't mind frozen French fries, we can pop some in the oven and that will be our supper."

"Sounds good to me," she said.

"There's time enough for you to take a shower if you'd like one now," he said.

"I would love a nice warm shower," she said.

"Then go for it," he said. He went out to start the grill, while she headed to the guest bath to do just that.

The water pressure was great and the warm water cascading over her head and down her back felt heavenly. She soaped herself well, scrubbing everywhere to get clean except for where her wound was bandaged.

Afterward, she felt like a new woman. Toweling off, she thought about what to wear. She'd been in such a hurry she hadn't brought anything in with her.

Poking her head out the door and looking up and down the hall, not seeing Destry, she hurried into her room and found a pair of yoga leggings and a big soft T-shirt.

The comfortable familiarity of her clothes wrapped around her, and she went back to hang her towel up and comb out her hair. She would leave it to dry naturally since they weren't going anywhere.

When she came back out to where Destry was, he had the food ready and plates and napkins outside on the table.

"Feel better?" he asked.

"Much," she said. "I can't tell you how good it is to be able to take showers again."

"I can imagine," he said, handing her a plate with a burger on a bun. "We'll get your wound cleaned tonight and put a fresh bandage on it."

"Thank you," she took the plate and piled some fries onto it before she sat down.

"Tell me more about what goes on at a rodeo," she said. "Is it the same every night?"

"With the PRCA, usually the sequence is, bareback tie down calf roping, saddle bronc bull dogging, barrel racing and bull riding."

"Wow," she said. "That's a lot."

"It is, but it goes fast," he said.

"Is it dangerous?"

"Rough stock is inherently more dangerous," he said.

"The more dangerous the horse or the bull, the higher the possible score. Scores are fifty percent the rider and fifty percent the animal. There are some bulls that have never been ridden to an entire eight second finish."

"I'm glad you're not risking your life with them anymore," she said.

"Darlin' you have no idea how many dangerous situations I've walked away from," he said.

"In your Delta job." She stated it, already knowing the answer before she heard it from him.

"Yes." That one-word answer and the set of his jaw told her he wasn't going to tell her any more about that part of his life.

Maybe he couldn't.

"Well, I'm glad you're not doing those things anymore and are making this ranch the new chapter in your life."

Scout came up to him and nudged his leg with the frisbee.

He looked down at his dog and grinned.

The border collie could be insatiable when it came to games of any kind. Frisbee throwing, tennis ball toss, or tug the rope. An active breed, Destry would have to tell him to rest, or he wouldn't.

"Drop," he said, and Scout dropped the frisbee.

Destry picked up the frisbee to toss it.

"I am enjoying this new chapter," he said, then he threw the frisbee and watched his dog race after it before turning to look at her. "And I'm enjoying your company."

"I'm enjoying yours too," she said.

She sat watching the two of them play.

It was amazing but nothing about being here felt awkward at all. Everything was calm and laid back, and he treated her as if she belonged here.

She didn't feel this at home with her own family. Though she missed them, she was much more comfortable here.

When they called it a night, she'd thought she would sleep well at the ranch house.

It was so quiet, there were no machine noises, no bright lights, and no nurses waking her. There weren't even any sounds of traffic or neighbors.

The only sounds were the ones Scout made as he moved about the house. Destry had said the border collie would settle down once he checked everything out and saw where they were.

He'd nosed open her door and stood there looking at her as if checking her out, before he padded over to Destry's room and went inside. His doggie bed was in there on the floor by the foot of Destry's bed.

Emma hadn't gotten up to close the door. She was already warm beneath the soft sheets and blanket and had been starting to doze off. She knew she could trust Destry, so she didn't mind the door being cracked.

But she did have to grin at the way Scout had checked on her, as if the dog were Nana, from Peter Pan, making sure the children were tucked in and sleeping.

She would have bet money that she would sleep like a baby.

But her dreams wouldn't let her.

They were chasing her again, and shooting.

She screamed and sat up in bed.

Destry came running, Scout right beside him.

"Pearl? Are you all right?" Destry asked. Seeing that she looked fine, he said, "It was another dream, wasn't it."

"Yes," she said, pushing her hair out of her face with a shaky hand. "They were coming for me again."

"You know you're safe here, and I'm not going to let anything happen to you." he said.

"I know," she said. "My shoulder, it hurts again, like when I was shot."

"Describe what it feels like," he said.

"A sharp pain, here," she pointed to a place on her shoulder, and he knew it was where the bullet had gone in.

"Yes, and what else?"

"The noise. It was so loud! So many bullets."

"They would have been very loud," he said.

"I wanted to cover my ears," she said.

"Of course," he said.

"Can you stay here with me for a little while?" she asked.

"Sure thing, darlin'," he said.

She scooted over and he sat on the bed next to her, on top of the covers and leaning against the headboard.

When Emma curled up next to him, he let his arm drop down around her.

It felt natural to feel his arm around her. Comforting.

"How did you end up in Montana?" he asked.

Emma began to talk, telling him everything, starting with her boss giving her the generous presents of the ticket and the new suitcase.

Destry stayed silent, listening as she went through the entire tale, ending with her going to the hospital. From there, he knew the rest.

He sat up with her and let her talk about the shooting on the highway, listening and lending his support, until she was all talked out.

Finally, she yawned.

"Think you'll be able to sleep now?" he asked.

"I can try," she said.

It wasn't long until she did.

Destry was the one left awake, puzzling over things.

Why was the cartel after her?

Did she know something they didn't want her to tell anyone? Did she have something they wanted?

She didn't know any cartel members, and she'd had no idea her boss had anything to do with them, or why they would come after her.

Occasionally, her boss had a meeting and wouldn't tell her where or with who. Just what time he'd be gone and when he'd be back. That had to have been when he'd been meeting with a cartel member.

But he wasn't representing any of them in court or she would have known that.

Representing someone in a court case wasn't something a lawyer could hide.

She was clueless as to what she might know.

The lawyer had clearly tried to protect her, sending her out of town. But the suitcase? Why add that? There had to be a reason.

Tomorrow, he wanted a look at that suitcase.

Chapter Eight

The next day he waited until they'd shared a breakfast of bacon and eggs with toast. Then he said, "That suitcase your boss gave you, I'd like to take a look at it."

"Why? It's empty," she said.

"Because it might not be completely empty."

"Oh." He eyes widened. "Okay, I hadn't thought of that."

He followed Emma into her bedroom.

As she opened the closet and bent to lift the suitcase, he said, "I'll get that," and lifted it for her, carrying it over to the bed.

He placed it on the bed and opened it.

At first glance, it looked empty. But then he ran his hand across every inch of the lining.

In a corner, beneath the lining, he felt it.

A fob. Small and easily missed. About the length of his thumbnail and half the size of it.

"You've found something?" she asked.

He nodded.

Taking out his pocketknife he made a slit in the fabric lining and then pushed the fob out until he held it in his hand.

The small black fob had to be what they were looking for.

She gasped. "That's what they think I have," she said. "That's why they're trying to kill me? This tiny little fob?"

"It's the information on it that they want."

"They can have it!" she said. "I don't even know what's on it and I don't want to know!"

He looked at her. "Do you mind if I keep this?"

"I don't want it!"

"Hey, calm down," he said. "It's just you and me here, and no one else knows we have this."

"I don't have it," she insisted, quieter now. "I never had it. I never touched it."

He slipped it into the pocket of his jeans. "Now it's gone. You don't ever have to see it again. I'll contact the Sheriff about it, see what he says."

"I should have known he didn't give me that suitcase just to be nice to me. He was trying to hide that thing! He put me in danger!"

"He did," Destry nodded. "And if he weren't dead already, I'd be having words with him."

The way he was clenching his fists, she suspected Destry would have been been doing more than talking to her boss.

"I don't want that suitcase," Emma said. "Please get rid of it too."

Destry picked the suitcase up by the handle. "This ought to go to the sheriff too. I'll put them away until he can come by to get them."

Emma watched him carry the suitcase out of the room.

At the doorway he turned and said, "Your boss may

have been trying to save your life, sending you out of town. And likely he did. But he was also trying to save his skin by passing that fob on with you."

She nodded, too mad at her boss right now to think about him or talk about it anymore.

Once Destry turned and took away the suitcase, she crawled on top of the bed, to rest on the quilt and her pillow.

She curled up on her side and stared at the books on the bedside table for a moment before reaching for one.

She needed to escape for a little while, into the world in one of her books. Choosing the cowboy romance, she opened it and started to read.

After he stowed the suitcase in his closet and was headed back down the hall, Destry paused at the doorway of her room and looked in, but seeing her there, reading, and decided not to speak so he wouldn't interrupt her.

She'd been wound up, understandably so, and it would do her good to relax a while. He'd noticed the three paperbacks piled up. Anyone who packed three paperbacks in a suitcase to go on a short vacation really liked to read. So, he would leave her to it.

There were plenty of things to do on a ranch and he needed to get on with them and to also work out some of his frustrations about a dead man who'd nearly gotten her killed.

He took Scout with him out to the barn to tackle chores that needed doing.

The more physical the better.

Other to come in for some water, and a quick ham sandwich, he kept busy working, and didn't see Emma the rest of the day. It seemed they were settling into a more normal routine after the initial getting to know you phase.

But there was still a lot about Emma that he didn't know. And he intended to address it this evening.

They'd just finished a supper of fajitas and were watching the sun set when Emma asked, "It sounded like you enjoyed being in the Army. So why did you get out?"

Destry paused scratching Scout's ear.

She was good at asking questions about him, but not so good at answering questions about herself. He determined to turn that around this evening.

"To help Gram with my grandfather," he said.

"Did he need help on his ranch?"

Destry shook his head no and looked away, remembering.

She waited for him to speak again.

"He had cancer."

"Oh no." Her heart went out to him.

"I moved back and helped Gram take care of him."

"That must have been hard," she said. "I'm so sorry."

"Six months of memories. No reason to be sorry."

Scout nudged him with his nose.

Destry began scratching his ear again.

"I'd have been off on missions and would have missed him."

"Then I'm glad," she said. "It's good you had your RN."

"I got it later. After he was gone."

He glanced around and she looked where he was looking and wondered what he was looking at.

"Family is everything," he said, "My grandfather helped me pick out this place."

"Family is important," she agreed. "The scenery is beautiful here," she said.

"What were your grandparents like?" he asked.

"My grandparents have both passed," she said.

"Grandpa was a big teaser, loved to tease me, and Grandmother made the best cakes. The old-fashioned kind you can't buy in a grocery store. Every year we got to pick our favorite and she would make it for our birthday."

"Your grandmother and my gram would have gotten along," he said. "What about your parents? How would you describe them?"

"My dad," she paused, thinking.

"Hardworking, quiet, honest, and fair. But my mother the home maker rules the roost, and he always let her have her way," she said.

He noted she'd placed her mother in the present tense. A slip up perhaps and he would bet that she was still living.

"Siblings?" he asked.

"Two brothers, I'm the youngest," she said.

Not once had she given a name. In the hospital she'd said she had no one to notify.

Maybe that meant she wasn't close to any of her family. Not that she didn't have one.

He hoped she would open up to him as she got to know him.

"My grandfather helped me chose the land, the layout of the barn, and the house."

"Did he help you build them?"

"By then he was too weak to do any work, but he gave great advice and enjoyed watching my progress."

"You have a lovely home," she said. "It's restful here."

"Thank you," he said. "I'm glad you find it restful."

They sat in companionable silence watching the sun go down and then walked with Scout on his nightly round of the property.

Then the stars were out, and they watched them twinkle in the night sky.

* * *

Dayton Ohio news wasn't picked up out in Billings, Montana, and Destry didn't watch TV much anyway, so neither of them saw the initial story that aired about a missing young woman named Emma Smith. And it would be days until they knew anything about the story.

Mrs. James Smith aka Olivia was filmed with tears in her eyes, begging for help.

"Our daughter is missing," she said. "The attorney she worked for was murdered and now she's missing." She clasped her hands in a prayer position. "Please. Help us find our daughter and bring her home safe."

The missing woman poster with Emma Smith's photo on it went out to many police departments and reached Bozeman, where she'd last been seen. But no one who saw it there made the connection between the missing woman and the woman who'd ended up in the Billings Clinic recently.

* * *

Brett Collier sat in his hotel room watching TV and drinking a glass of bourbon when he saw the news clip and heard Emma Smith's name. He turned the volume up to make sure he'd heard correctly.

Mrs. James Smith, mother of Emma Smith, was begging for help to find their daughter.

He watched till the end of the clip and then sat his glass down reached for his phone.

The photo shown was of Emma Smith, the woman he'd sat next to on the plane.

Where Emma went, after leaving the airport with the man who had met her there, he had no idea, but he knew every nugget of information could help them reconstruct her actions and help them find her.

He had a description of the man, the limo, and remembered the license plate number.

He hoped the pretty lady was still alive.

As a DEA analyst, he might be able to help. He'd had Army training in intel, and once out had joined the DEA and received further training.

He would do all he could to help find Emma.

His first call was to the Bozeman police department as that was the last town he'd seen her in. His second call would be to the DEA offices where other analysts worked.

The cartel also trafficked women.

He prayed they hadn't gotten their hands on Emma.

Since Brett made the call, Emma's picture, which had been shared with police officers in Ohio and on the law enforcement computer systems had reached Billings, Montana for the police department to look at.

Emma Smith looked remarkably like Pearl Hays.

"She had no I.D.," Lieutenant Kelly said as he looked at the photo. "It has to be the same woman, traveling under an assumed name."

"Her mother said they received a package mailed to her at their address containing her driver's license and credit cards."

"She was on the run," detective Charles O'Malley said.

Sheriff Colt knew he needed to talk to Destry.

He went outside to his car and using his cell phone dialed the number.

"I need to meet with you," he said when Destry picked up.

"When and where?" Destry asked.

The sheriff gave him the info and then hung up.

Destry would meet with him in a couple of hours, and he couldn't bring Emma. "I'm headed out to get some supplies," he told her. "You'll stay here with Scout."

"I'll play frisbee with him," she said.

"You know he'll like that," he said. "Call if you need me."

"Okay."

* * *

Once Destry met Sheriff Colt at a local gas station, Sheriff Colt didn't waste words.

"There's a missing woman named Emma Pearl Smith who is a dead ringer for our Pearl," he said. "She's already tried to disappear once by changing her name to Pearl Hayes."

"What?" Destry said.

The sheriff showed Destry the photo that everyone had seen blasted all over the news.

"This is Emma. Her mother released this photo to the press. Alerts have gone out all over."

"Damn it," Destry said. "With facial recognition systems everywhere, it's almost impossible to hide out in public."

He was peeved that she'd lied to him. He understood why, but he still wasn't happy about it. He'd known she was lying but he'd thought she might open up to him about it once she was staying with him.

So far it hadn't happened.

He and Emma were going to have a good long talk once he got home. He would push her to tell him everything. Every detail, because he needed those details to help him keep her safe.

When he arrived home, she was tossing the frisbee for Scout. He hoped she hadn't been doing it ever since he left.

Border collies would not stop working to rest unless they were told too.

He took the frisbee from Scout when his dog brought it back. "Scout, water," he said.

Scout wagged his tail, panting and then went to his water bowl to drink.

Destry pulled a chair around so that the two chairs were facing each other and then said, "Have a seat."

She sat, stretching her legs out and said, "Your dog can wear a girl out."

"Woman," he said.

"Girl, woman," she shrugged.

He sat in the chair across from her. "We need to talk."

Her jaw dropped and her eyes became guarded. "What about?"

"About the fact that you lied to me about who you are, Emma Smith, from Dayton, Ohio."

Her face turned red, and she stood feeling like she needed to bolt.

"Sit down," he said. "And start talking. I'm here to protect you, so you need to start being honest with me."

She nodded but didn't speak.

"Start at the beginning, back in Dayton, and tell me everything that's happened since."

Emma took a shaky breath and began.

When she was done, it felt as if she'd lost thirty pounds. She'd finally told someone the whole story of what had happened. Not just the part of it that she had shared with him before. Now she wasn't the only one who knew.

"Mr. Smalls didn't make it," she said. "He's the only one who knew." She looked up into Destry's eyes. "And now there's you. Don't you die on me too."

"I assure you, Emma, that I am a very hard man to kill."

She blinked. For a moment she'd forgotten about his special training. "Mr. Smalls had been a professional boxer," she said. "He was tough too."

"Boxing is just one skill set," Destry said. "I have many to choose from. And my one job right now is to protect you. But for this to work well, I need you to promise me. No more lies. Not with me."

She nodded her agreement. "No more lies."

* * *

Destry was in the shower, had just stepped in and turned the water on, while Emma was in the kitchen washing dishes in the sink, when there was a knock on the back door.

Startled, Emma whirled.

Someone is here! What do I do? If I move into another room, they'll see me through the window in the door!

She froze.

The door started opening.

Her eyes widened.

They're coming in!

Destry was still in the shower, by the sound of the water running.

Where's Scout?

Destry had let him outside before he went to shower. But Scout hadn't barked.

"Hello, Destry dear," a female voice called as she walked through the back door. "Are you in here? I looked in the barn ..."

A short gray-haired woman with wide blue eyes, wearing glasses, stood just inside the door, looking at Emma in wide eyed surprise, stopped her in her tracks, pausing whatever she would've said next.

"Oh my," she said. "I've come at a bad time. Didn't know Destry had a lady friend over." She smiled wide. "I'm Destry's grandmother, Claire Falls Walsh."

Gram. This was Destry's gram.

The tension drained out of Emma, leaving her feeling limp.

Gram was a sweet little old lady, not a cartel bad guy.

Emma dried her hands on a towel and said, "Nice to meet you Mrs. Walsh." She stepped toward her and held out her hand. "I've heard so much about you."

An answering twinkle came into Mrs. Walsh's eyes as she shook her hand. "And you are a complete surprise! I haven't heard a thing about you, my dear. But we can fix that over a slice of pie."

Pie? We don't have any pie.

"I only baked one, now, mind," Mrs. Walsh said. "It's in my car, along with a few casseroles, and a gallon of tea. That boy never has enough food in the house, especially for company!"

She gave Emma a beaming smile, clearly pleased to see that Destry had female company.

"That's very thoughtful of you," Emma said. She wished her grandmother were still alive. Destry's was clearly a sweetheart.

"Destry usually brings the things in." His gram listened for a moment, and hearing the shower, she got an even more delighted look in her eyes.

Emma could see her mind working.

Him in the shower and me barefoot in his kitchen doing the dishes. That must be looking very domestic.

"Oh, well, we needn't wait for him," Emma said. "I can carry your things in," She walked over and slipped on her sandals which stood near the back door.

Mrs. Walsh followed Emma out and they walked to a little white Toyota Corolla parked near the barn. Mrs. Walsh opened the door and reached in for her pie which was sitting in a box on the passenger seat.

"Is that a homemade chocolate cream pie?" Emma asked.

"Yes, my dear it is," Mrs. Walsh said. "I have the pie. If you could carry one of my casseroles, that would be a help."

"Of course," Emma said.

Each casserole was inside a quilted carry-all. Emma had never seen anything like it.

The carriers had handles, so she reached in, grasped one carrier in each hand, and then using one hip, closed the door so bugs wouldn't get in.

Or hungry border collies. She had no idea if Scout would eat people food, but most dogs she'd known, did.

She followed Mrs. Walsh back to the kitchen. Setting both casseroles on the counter, she watched Mrs. Walsh put the pie on the table. Then Mrs. Walsh got out two small plates, a knife, and two forks. "If you would get the milk, dear," she said to Emma.

"Of course," Emma said. She went to the fridge for the half gallon of milk and then got out two glasses.

Taking them to the table, she watched Mrs. Walsh dividing the pie into large slices.

"About half that, for me," Emma said.

"Oh no, my dear, this is not a half slice of pie conversation," Destry's gram said. "And it's chocolate. You'll want the full experience."

Emma couldn't help but laugh.

Down the hall, she heard a door close, and noticed the water had been turned off.

"What's funny, Pearl?" Destry called out. "What am I missing out on?"

His gram put her hand over her mouth and giggled. Then she held one finger up with a low, "Shhh."

She really is adorable, his little gram. And wasn't he going to be surprised!

"Oh, just a little surprise," Emma said, and giggled.

Mrs. Walsh shook her finger at Emma twice in a gesture that said naughty, naughty.

Destry rounded the corner and stopped.

Seeing his gram, his face broke out in a huge smile that could have lit the room.

"Gram!" He opened his arms wide and went in to give her a big hug.

Mrs. Walsh laughed and hugged him right back, rocking him from side to side with a big squeeze.

Watching them made Emma's heart happy.

When they broke loose, his gram sat again, and said, "We were just having pie. Will you join us?"

"You know I will," he winked at her. Then he went to get another fork and came back to the table to sit down.

She gave him a look. "Where is your plate, young man?"

He laughed and went to get a plate. "Right here," he said, waving the plate. Then he came back and sat down.

"That's my boy," she said with a big smile as she dished him out a generous slice of pie. "He's been doing that since he was five. I don't know what I'd do if he started off with more than a fork."

They all laughed.

"Was he mischievous as a boy?" Emma asked, wondering if she would hear tales of Destry's past.

"Very," Mrs. Walsh said. "And he was the daredevil, always climbing things and trying things. Just to see if he could. I thought it wouldn't get worse than that and then he joined the Delta Force, and I worried he'd never come home again."

"And then I did," he said. "And I'm here now."

"That you are, my boy," she patted his hand. "And I couldn't be happier. Unless you have some news to tell me?" She looked back and forth between the two of them.

"Nothing to tell, gram," he said.

"Well, then, let's just enjoy our pie," she said.

They all took their first bites and were quiet for a minute.

The burst of flavor across her tongue made Emma close her eyes.

When she opened them, Destry was watching her, and his gram was watching them both with a quiet smile.

"This is the best chocolate pie I've ever had," she said.

"I'd have to agree," Destry said. "No one tops grams chocolate pie."

"Why thank you both," Mrs. Walsh said. "Now Pearl, that's such a pretty name. Tell me about you. Where are you from, and how did you and Destry meet?"

Destry raised an eyebrow at Pearl, the minute he heard her name, likely wondering why she hadn't given his gram the name they'd made up for her to use if she met anyone new.

She gave him a look back, wishing she could say, you called my name down the hallway, Mr. So don't give me that look.

But she couldn't say that. And she needed to answer his gram and come up with believable lies.

"I was in the Billings Clinic," she said. "Had a surgery on my shoulder. Destry was my nurse."

His gram clasped her hands together with a look of joy. "Fated mates."

"Now, gram, this is not one of your romance novels," Destry said. "Our meeting was a normal, expected in a hospital kind of meeting. And we are friends, not dating."

Her face fell a little, but she regained a happy expression soon afterward. "You should use your tickets and take her to the rodeo," she said.

"Actually, we'd already decided that he'd take me," Emma said. "After I'd told him I'd never seen a rodeo."

"Well now, that is wonderful," Mrs. Walsh clasped her hands together. "I know of no one better than Destry to teach you all about rodeo. He was quite the one to beat, in his prime."

"He was?"

"All those trophies and awards in the other room tell the stories," Mrs. Walsh said. "The only things not on display are his belt buckles and cash awards. You should ask him to see his belt buckles. He could model them for you." She grinned. "Best way for you to see them."

"Gram..." Destry warned.

"You must bring your new friend to the family barbecue," she said, quickly changing the subject.

Emma started to object, but before she could, Mrs.

Walsh held up her hand. "Now, no excuses. Everyone will want to meet you. It's the day before the rodeo he's taking you to, so I'll expect to see you both there."

Pushing her next bite of pie around on her plate, now that she was feeling pressured, and knowing she was supposed to keep a low profile, Emma focused on her pie and said, "Tell me more about the family barbecue."

"We've held the family barbecue ever since my grandfather came to Wyoming and built the home place. It became our family reunion over the years as the family spread out on the globe."

"That's a wonderful tradition," Emma said.

"It is," Mrs. Walsh agreed. Then she turned to Destry. "Have you heard from Jake? Is he coming out this year?"

"I've talked to him, and he'll try to make it, if he can."

"Destry's cousin Jake is a Navy SEAL." Mrs. Walsh said. "We never know when he's coming or going. Like Destry used to be before he came home for good."

"Do you remember the year Jake showed up halfway through dessert, on an old borrowed Harley," Destry said. "To surprise you."

She laughed. "It was my birthday. The big eight-o. How could I ever forget that one? Best gift ever."

"Everyone made it to that one," Destry said.

"That's wonderful," Emma said. "Is the barbecue always on your birthday?"

"Most years," Mrs. Walsh said. "But it was held on that weekend long before I was born and became a family tradition, before I was even a thought."

They'd all finished their pie slices, and she laid her fork down. "This year, I'll look forward to you joining us, Pearl. Now I'm going to head on home before it gets dark, and leave you two to put the food away."

They all stood. "It was nice to meet you," Emma said.

Mrs. Walsh grasped Emma's hand. "It's been a pleasure, my dear," she said. Then she squeezed her hand. "I'm looking forward to seeing you again."

Destry walked his gram out to her car and told her he needed to talk to her privately about a secret.

He came back in carrying the sun tea. "Sorry about that," he said. "I would have told her I had a guest but couldn't share that over the phone and I haven't had time to go over there to talk to her about you.."

"It's okay," Emma said. "Though she did scare me half to death when she came in. I thought they'd found me. And Scout didn't bark!"

He placed his warm hands on her shoulders, which lost some of their tension. "Better now?"

"Yes," she said. "The pie helped." She gave him a smile. "Your gram is so sweet."

"Gram's pie always helps," he said. "And I agree. She's a sweetheart. But if you get on her bad side, she'll show you the stern bad ass underneath all that sweetness."

"Well, I can't imagine getting on her bad side," Emma said.

"Few people have," he said. "But if they do, she will cut that off fast."

"So, this family reunion picnic," Emma said. "Is it going to be safe for me to go there?"

"Gram isn't going to tell anyone about you," he said. "I'll find out who's going and if they're bringing any extras.

"With my family, if I say tight lips then that's what we get. Between Jake and me, they're used to not being able to tell people where we are, or what we are doing. Saying SEAL or Delta must be enough. My family is well trained.

But I can't say that of others they might bring with them. We'll need to know the guest list before we commit."

"Oh, but you should go," she said. "It's your family reunion and your grams birthday."

"I'll get Jake to talk to her, after he gets in," Destry said. "He's planning to be there unless something happens."

They sat outside, watching the stars when suddenly Emma spoke. "Does it get lonely out here?"

"Sometimes," he said.

He hadn't noticed just how lonely until her bright smiling presence had entered his house.

She brightened up a room just by walking into it.

It was a little alarming just how glad he was for her company. How attached he'd become to Pearl Hayes.

If her circumstances were different, he could see them staying together and growing closer. But if her circumstances were different, she likely wouldn't be here.

It's best to focus on what is. Here in this moment, today. Tomorrow was always a wild card. Even in the best circumstances life could turn on a dime when you least expected it. When you grew soft and unprepared.

Chapter Nine

As they drove to his Gram's house for the family reunion Barbecue, Emma was nervous to meet the rest of his family.

A dark-haired man came around the corner, carrying a large serving plate piled with corn on the cob, for Gram as she hurried along beside him with a bowl of homemade coleslaw.

Her eyes lit as soon as she saw them. "Emma!" she said, "I'm so glad you came with Destry. Now you can meet the rest of the family."

She set the bowl down on the table. "This handsome fellow helping me is Destry's cousin, Jake Summers."

Dark intense eyes met hers.

Goodness, are all the men in this family tall, handsome and fit?

If she wasn't so attracted to Destry, Jake would surely have turned her head.

"Ma'am," he said, tipping his hat, now that he'd set down the corn. "Nice to meet you."

Nice to meet you as well," she said.

"Come along and help me in the kitchen, dear," Gram said. "I've just a few more things to bring out."

"Happy to help," Emma said.

The men watched them go and then Jake said, "Cuz, she's a pretty one."

"I agree," Destry said.

"Gram told me what happened to her," Jake said.

"She's lucky to be alive," Destry said.

"Now she's at your place," Jake said. "Any sign of the cartel in your area?"

"So far, no," Destry said. "I hope it stays that way."

"Me too," Jake said. "If you need me, call."

"I will," Destry said. "Thanks, man."

"No problem," Jake said.

They watched the women come back out, Emma carrying Gram's potato salad and Gram carrying a large pan of Texas sheet cake that her mother had passed down.

Once the food was all on the table, Gram said, "Attention everyone! I'd like everyone to welcome Emma, Destry's guest."

As introductions went all around, Destry's parents, Henry and Bonnie Walsh welcomed her as if she were one of their own.

Surrounded by the other thirteen members of his family, she could see where Destry got many of his qualities.

She met his parents, his gram, his sister Tammy and her husband and two boys, his aunt and uncle with their three sons, and his cousin Jake. She wasn't sure she would remember all their names.

"Come and get it," Henry Walsh called, from over by the grill. "Ribs are ready!"

Destry and Emma got plates and went over to the grill.

"Ribs, or burgers," Henry Walsh said. "You can choose one or choose both."

"I'd never be able to eat all those ribs and a burger too," Emma said as she eyed them trying to decide.

Ribs were messy and she'd be eating them in front of Destry and all these people she'd just met, so she was almost ready to choose a burger, though she was really wanting to try the ribs.

"Here you go," Henry placed ribs and a burger on her plate. "If you can't eat all your ribs, Destry will help you polish them off." He gave her a wink.

Destry didn't even have to tell his dad what he wanted, as Mr. Walsh put a rack of ribs on his plate.

"Thanks dad," Destry said. "Looks good."

Emma walked with him over to the table laden with food, looked at it all and said, "There's no way a little of everything will fit on our plates."

"We'll need a second trip to try everything," Destry agreed. "I'm having coleslaw, if you want a bite of mine."

"Then I'll get the potato salad, and we can do the same."

She skipped the corn on the cob.

In case something got caught in her teeth. She didn't want to embarrass herself.

They found their seats and then Destry brought her a glass of lemonade and himself a beer.

"I'm surprised you didn't ask me if I wanted a beer," she said.

"I would have, but one of those meds you're still on doesn't mix with alcohol."

"Oh, I hadn't thought of that," she said.

"You've only got a few days left of it and then you can have as many beers as you want."

"I'm not much of a beer drinker," she said. "But a glass of wine is nice."

"Good to know," Destry said. He took a swallow and then set his beer can down. "I'm driving, so one is my limit."

She took a bite of her ribs. They were tender and tasty but not what she'd expected. "These don't taste like pork."

"That's because they're beef," he said with a grin. "Remember we're in cattle country. And some ranches have buffalo."

"They eat buffalo?"

"Sure do," he said. "Just like the tribes have always done. It's leaner and healthier for you."

"I'll have to try it sometime," Emma said.

"Yes, you will," Destry said with a nod. "My family has stuck to raising beef. But I know a rancher who raises buffalo."

"That's family beef you're eating," Mr. Walsh said.

"It is?"

"Yep."

"These ribs are delicious," Emma told him.

"Glad you're enjoying them." Mr. Walsh walked past them and sat down to eat now that the grilling was done, and the meat handed out.

Destry watched as Emma took another bite which left a bit of barbecue sauce on her lips.

He smiled and watched her eat, as the urge to kiss her nudged him.

It wasn't something he'd do in the middle of a meal, or in the middle of his family gathering, so acting on this urge would have to wait. But he could watch her and think about it.

Their first kiss had been so memorable, he couldn't get it

off his mind. The way her lips had felt beneath his, and the taste of her.

Since then, he'd found his gaze drifting to her lips, often. Usually at the most inopportune times, such as right now, when he couldn't do anything about it.

And when her gaze landed on his lips, he knew she was thinking about it too.

After they'd finished eating and had helped to clear the tables and do the dishes, Gram insisted on sending leftovers home with them.

Soon they were driving back home, the sun had set, and the stars were out.

"Want to sit out back and enjoy the night air when we get home?" he asked.

Their nightly talks beneath the stars were becoming a habit he looked forward to each night. He hoped she was enjoying that as much as he was.

"Yes," Emma said. "I'm much too full to get ready for bed. And Scout will want to run."

"He will," Destry said. "What did you think of our family reunion?" He asked.

"It's like I've found a new family out here," Pearl said. "Everyone in your family is so nice."

"I think gram would adopt you if she could," he said.

"I just wish I could let my family know where I am, and that I'm okay," she sighed. "I wish I could talk to mother and dad, and both my brothers."

"You'd put them and yourself in danger, if they're being watched," Destry said. "Phone lines can be tapped."

"I know," she said with a soft sigh.

* * *

July 3rd came and with it, her excitement about going to see the rodeo had reached a peak.

As they drove through Cody, on the main road which led through town, she could see old buildings, and the new ones built for the tourists.

Cody had always been a town for travelers, and as the birthplace of Buffalo Bill's Wild West Rodeo Show, still the rodeo capitol of the world, the rodeo in Cody had always been a main draw for tourists.

"You said Cody was near the east gate of Yellowstone," she said.

"That's the closest gate," he said.

"Will we see Yellowstone?"

"No, we'd drive west to see Yellowstone," he said, "Through a couple of tunnels and past the dam."

"There's a dam?"

"Yep. The Buffalo Bill Dam. I'll have to show it to you some other time," he said. "It's something to see."

"This whole town," she waved her hand at the Buffalo Bill Museum with its statues and a chuck wagon out front, "Is something to see."

"It is," he said, "If you've never seen it."

"I suppose you're used to all this, growing up out here," she said. "It's probably old hat to you."

"The Cody stampede is never old," he said. "Always exciting, no matter how many times I go."

"Oh, that's good," she said. "It would be fun to stay here, just at the entrance to Yellowstone."

"If you wanted to do that, there's Pahaska Tepee Resort which was Buffalo Bills Original Lodge. It's only two miles outside Yellowstone."

"That sounds like fun," she said.

"It will be booked full this weekend, even though it's an

hour's drive from the rodeo. Everything in town will be booked."

"So, is this the height of the tourist season here?"

"It is. Normally I don't head into town, just head to the rodeo, but I want to take you out for the Mexican food you've been craving. There's a little family-owned Mexican place on the way. Often there's a line, so we'll go early to get in and then head to the rodeo."

"I'll bet the line is long. And they probably stay busy this weekend."

"Actually, they close at six pm. Like I said, it's a family business."

"I wonder why they wouldn't stay open this weekend to make more money?"

"Family probably wants to go to the rodeo."

"Oh! I didn't think of that."

"And it's their regular business hours."

"Well, I can hardly wait." Her stomach grumbled, echoing that statement.

Michael's Tacos stood on the left-hand side of the road. To the right side was a beautiful view of the mountains in the distance with the early evening sun shining behind them.

Destry pulled into the parking lot, near the entrance, and parked. He got out, came around to open her door, and then gave her his hand to help her down.

She wasn't used to stepping on running boards before getting out of a vehicle, but she was glad they were there, as she was too short to easily get in and out without stepping on one. Her left shoulder was still healing, so she used her right hand to grip the hand bar to get in and out.

She appreciated his help, as placing her hand in his, she

held on, stepped onto the running board, and then stepped down to the concrete.

There was indeed even moved forward.

She couldn't help but keep looking at the mountain scene before her, and realized he'd said something she missed.

"Sorry," she said, giving him her attention again. She gestured with her hand to the view across the street of the mountains. "It's just so beautiful, I got distracted."

The line moved until it was their turn, and they could move beyond the rope, to a table.

Once they were seated, the waitress asked. "Are you ready to order?"

"Yes," Destry said and nodded to Emma to go first.

"I'd like two enchiladas, one cheese and one chicken," she said. "And just rice, no beans. And water to drink." With the medicine they had her on, she couldn't have a margarita.

"I'll have your big burrito with beef," Destry said, " Wait until you see the size of it." He winked at Emma.

She blushed a little and wondered if he was making an innuendo. Playing along, she said, "I can't wait to see it and find out if your claims are true." Then she winked back at him.

He chuckled.

"To drink?" The waitress asked.

"A cola," he said.

The big burrito when it came, took up the whole plate. Another plate held his side dishes. Her meal was also a good-sized serving. Both hungry, they dug in. Destry shared his burrito with her so she could try it, insisting there was plenty for two.

Finally, they were both full, just in time to head over to the rodeo.

"Everything was delicious," she said.

"I'm glad you enjoyed it," he said.

Once he paid the bill, they headed out and got back into the truck. He handed her a mint once she got in.

"Thank you," she said.

Back in the truck, they drove down the road again.

As she looked from one side to the other, to take everything in, Destry said, "It will be on the right."

This made sense because to the left, behind the hotels and restaurants and shops, was a tall hill.

"There's a rodeo here every night, from June through August, and any cowboy or cowgirl can enter to test their skill against the others. Fourth of July weekend events are the biggest and will draw top cowboys from all over the world."

The Cody rodeo arena stood on a large section of land at the edge of town past the Mexican restaurant. With mountains to the west of the stadium, there were no buildings to clutter the landscape.

You could feel you were out west, with few people around.

Cars and trucks to the side and the back of the stadium said otherwise.

Horse trailers and small RVs were parked behind the stadium arena.

People were parking and walking toward the ticket takers at the entrance.

Destry parked his truck and got out, just as she reached for her door to open it.

She had the door halfway open as he came around the front of the truck, and he opened it up all the way and said,

"No ma'am," with a slight shake of his head. "Out here we like to open doors for our women."

His words sunk in, and gave her a warm feeling, though she knew he meant they opened doors for all the ladies.

Not that she was his woman.

A small part of her deep down inside wished she was.

He was kind, caring, patient, and very much a gentleman.

She liked being treated like a lady.

"Thank you," she said, as she stepped out and stood, really meaning it, not just being polite. "It's nice." She smiled.

"No problem." He smiled back.

She doubted he was thinking of her in the way she inwardly wished he was.

He was just being polite and a gentleman.

She shouldn't read more into it than that.

The sun going down in the west behind the mountains leant an orange glow across the stadium and grounds around it.

They pulled in around the back of the large lot, which was filled with trucks, horse trailers, and even a few RVs.

She noticed the many different types of license plates.

"They come from all over," she said.

"Yes," he nodded as he pulled up in between two other trucks.

"Big prize money this weekend," he said. "You'll see cowboys from all over who've worked hard to be able to compete here this weekend."

He parked and came around to open her door as she waited, finally getting used to his gentlemanly behavior.

Even though they hadn't been dating before tonight's official first date, he'd kept up the gentlemanly behavior.

A far cry from the men she'd gone out with, who hadn't kept the practice up beyond the first date.

She'd been staying with Destry for over a month, and he showed no sign of changing how he treated her.

Emma reminded herself again that he'd already had the tickets and maybe this wouldn't have been a date if he hadn't already had them.

But her body wasn't listening, as his hand now rested on the small of her back, to guide her to where the ticket takers were.

The response of her body told her otherwise.

Surely, she wasn't imagining the way their bodies responded to each other.

That pull between them.

His voice alone could pull her there.

He wasn't a touchy-feely kind of guy, and his touch had never seemed inappropriate.

She liked his warm hand on her lower back, making her feel safe and protected as they walked forward.

Several cowboys glanced at her, and a few nodded to him.

His hand at her back sent a 'this one is with me' message to the other men.

Maybe if other guys thought she was Destry's girlfriend, then none of them would approach her.

She wasn't ready for strange men to be asking her out.

Even if they were handsome cowboys.

But Destry, she knew him, so it felt good to go on a first date with him, and she was excited about the rodeo.

As Destry handed in their tickets, the crowd of people now behind him made her nervous.

"Come on," he said, taking her elbow. "Our seats are on the other side."

"Okay," she said, relieved to move away from the crowd.

He led her to the stadium seating on the other side, and down to the bottom rows.

With surprise she realized they'd be seated down in front.

"Oh, we're down front," she said.

"Best place," he said. "You'll get to see the animals and riders up close. Those shoots are where the animals will come out."

Their seats were right above the shoots.

"Oh, that's exciting," she said, sending him a big smile.

He smiled back at her. "Settle in," he said, now that they'd reached their seats.

She smiled back and settled in.

Once she had, he handed her the program.

Now that the rodeo arena seats were filling, the noise and commotion both excited her and made her nervous. Though Destry had assured her that she'd be safe, and she trusted him, she couldn't help the tension that crept into her body from being in such a large crowd.

This was the first she'd been out in public, at a large public event since the shooting. Fear of being seen hovered in the back of her mind. She was used to being hidden, not seen. And there were still bad men out there who wanted to kill her.

"Hey," Destry said, settling his hand on her knee. "You doing okay?"

She nodded, not wanting to give voice to her fears.

He began pointing out where things would happen and what those things were, as he answered questions about the events listed in the program.

A skinny man in a cowboy hat came up to them. "Hey, Destry," he said. "Good to see you."

"Likewise," Destry said. "This is Helen Jones."

He introduced her, using the name they'd agreed upon since she couldn't use Emma Smith or Pearl Hayes.

The skinny cowboy wore boots, jeans, a cowboy hat, and a belt with a silver buckle.

Briefly she thought the man should've been named slim.

"Nice to meet you, Helen," the man shook her hand. "I'm Chris Marks."

"it's nice to meet you, Chris," she said, shaking his hand. "This is my first rodeo."

He whistled. "Who-ee, that's a great way to start," he said. Then he glanced at Destry. "You're going to spoil her for other rodeos after this one."

Destry smiled. "I figured she could use some spoiling."

"Well done," Chris clapped Destry on the shoulder. Then he addressed Emma "If y'all need anything, let me know."

"I might ask you to keep her company later, if I have to step away," Destry said.

"That would be my pleasure," Chris said with a nod. "Just let me know."

Another man came up to them on the other side, and Chris tipped his hat before walking away.

Goodness. These mannerly cowboys could make a woman feel special. I dare not get used to this. It will be different when I go back home to Ohio. Some day.

An older man in a brown Stetson wearing jeans, cowboy boots and a denim shirt sat on the other side of Emma. He nodded and said, "Destry."

Destry grinned back at him. "Wyatt Whitt, this is my girlfriend, Helen Jones."

She smiled at the older man. "Nice to meet you," she said.

"The pleasure is mine, little lady," Mr. Whitt said.

The announcer welcomed everyone, and the crowd quieted down to listen.

First several horses and riders came in bearing the American flag.

The national anthem was announced and as it played, everyone in the stands stood with their hands over their hearts to sing.

The sight and sound was so moving, so patriotic, that Emma got goosebumps on her arms and the back of her neck, and tears came to her eyes.

Once they finished singing, she rubbed at her eyes to clear her vision.

As they sat down again, Destry took her hand in his and gave it a squeeze.

A tingle spread from her hand up her arm.

Best to go along and enjoy this, whatever this is.

So, she simply sent him a smile.

"Let me know if you have any questions," he said.

Boy did she ever. But not ones she could ask him. So, she just nodded.

Chapter Ten

"Comfortable?" Destry asked.

"Yes," Emma said. She took the program from him.

The front of the program said Buffalo Bill annual Cody Stampede. PRCA Rodeo July 1 – 2- 3 – 4 the show of all shows Cody, Wyoming, the Rodeo Capitol of the World.

Beneath that was an image of a cowboy with one arm flung out to the side and the other hand gripping the ropes while riding a bucking horse whose rear feet were in the air, trying to buck the cowboy off.

Below the cowboy in large bold print, it read "400,000.00 total purse."

Pursing her lips, she blew out a low whistle. "No wonder all the cowboys come to compete here this weekend."

"Not all of them darlin,' Wyatt Witt said. "Only the ones who have advanced to be able to compete here. They work all year to achieve that."

"So just being here to compete is a big deal," she said.

"Yes, ma'am," Mr. Whitt said with a nod. "It is."

"This is my first rodeo," she said.

He chuckled.

She supposed it was because of the phrase 'This isn't my first rodeo' which was used so often.

"Don't say that too loud," a man behind them, wearing a black cowboy hat, said with a laugh.

"I'm not embarrassed to be new at something," she said. "Everyone starts somewhere."

"Yes, ma'am, you are correct," Mr. Whitt said. "What JB McGown here is referring to, is the fact that many cowboys would love to teach you about rodeo." He laughed. "About the only thing keeping you from being swarmed by cowboys, is that you're here with Destry."

Destry slid his arm around her shoulders, and said, "Helen is my date for this evening, if anyone is asking."

"You know they are," JB said, "Ma'am," he looked at her as he stood and then gave her a nod and then walked away.

"JB is a bigger gossip than a woman at a beauty salon," Destry said with a chuckle. "Just a matter of minutes before they all know you're with me."

"Is all this necessary? This is only our first date," Emma said. "It's not like we've been going out."

"Yes, it is," Destry said. "Instead of fending off their attention, you can relax and enjoy the rodeo."

Lowering her voice to a whisper, she said, "I like being your date."

She blushed waiting for his answer.

His eyes lit, the skin around them wrinkled, and his lips spread in a smile that lit up his whole face.

Sitting this close to him, she noticed every little movement across his face and realized once again how handsome he was, especially here in his element.

Her rodeo cowboy.

"It's my pleasure," he said. "I want your first rodeo to be as memorable as our first date."

She nodded and smiled back at him, while thinking, *it already is.*

He tapped her program. "Open it up, and let's see who's on the roster this evening."

She opened the program, which was the size of a magazine and just as jam filled with colorful ads. A major cola company took over the whole first page in full color with a picture of a thirst-quenching drink.

She swallowed.

"Are you thirsty? I can go get us some drinks and snacks," he said.

Clearing her sudden dry throat, she said, "Yes, I am. A little. Didn't realize how dry my mouth was."

He gave a small frown.

"If your mouth is dry, you're already dehydrated," he said. "Remember what I told you about drinking water?"

"Yes," she said. "I wouldn't mind a cola."

"Water first, cola after," he said. "A cola won't hydrate you, it does the opposite. I'll get us a couple of waters for now. Hungry?"

"Not really. Dinner was so filling."

"Yes, it was."

"I'll get us something to drink," he said. "Be right back."

He stood and went over to a woman who was selling drinks to people in the stands.

She eagerly looked through the program while she waited on him to come back. Reading the schedule, she got excited.

There were so many cowboys and cowgirls to see in action. She kept reading.

Event No. 1 - Grand Entry

Event No. 2 - Bareback Bronc Riding listed twelve riders and twelve horses.

She smiled at the names which were creative and fun.

Event No. 3 - Steer Wrestling sponsors were a radio network and a beverage company. There were ten wrestlers listed, but the steers weren't named.

Event No. 4 - was a Special Presentation and Event No. 5 was a Clown Act "Brody Buckley"

Event No. 6 - Team Roping listed ten teams of two.

Event No. 7 - Saddle Bronc Riding sponsored by a beer company and a sports medicine doc. Eleven riders and eleven broncs were listed.

Event No. 8 - Specialty Act listed a male rider and a female sponsored by a boot company and the Buffalo Bill Center of the West

Event No. 9 - Breakaway Roping sponsored by another beer company and a local hotel. Ten contestants competing.

Event No. 10 - Tie Down Roping sponsored by a pizza restaurant and another hotel. Ten ropers competing.

Event No. 11 - Women's Barrel Racing sponsored by the local hospital. Ten women competing.

Event No. 12 - Bull Riding sponsored by a bank and a hotel. Fourteen Riders listed and twelve bulls.

She wondered if there weren't enough bulls for every rider and maybe some of the bulls would be ridden twice. She would have to ask Destry.

The breeze had died and now it felt like the heat had risen. Her head was hot, so she took her new cowboy hat off and lifted her hair off her neck, hoping for a cooling breeze to come along soon.

Destry saw her, hatless, as he turned to head back with their drinks, and narrowed his eyes.

What the hell was she thinking?

She might be recognized.

He moved swiftly back to her side. "Put your hat on," he said. "Someone might see you and recognize you."

She put the hat back on.

Hopefully she'd done it in time.

Now he was tense as he scanned their surroundings.

Anyone in this crowd could have seen her.

No one appeared to be watching her now. He tried to relax and sent her a smile.

They watched the bareback riders getting ready and had a good view from their vantage point.

As she looked down, she said, "That looks like a suitcase handle."

"That's called the rigging body," Destry said. "That rigging' he's grasping is a custom made individually fitted piece depending on the riders handhold, the width, length, thickness, and the space between it. And if he's right-handed or left-handed."

"Are the gloves custom too?"

"It's a thick glove, fits into the handle with rosin that activates with heat to create a tight fit."

"What's rosin?"

"It's a sticky glue-like powder," he said.

The saddle bronc riders were getting ready.

She watched as they put the saddles on.

"Bronc saddles are sometimes called association saddles," Destry said. "They must meet certain specifications given by the PRCA.

"So will all the saddles be the same?"

"The specs must be the same, but riders have different needs. A bronc rider's style depends a great deal upon the saddle he uses. So, finding one that fits him is important. The difference between a bronc saddle and a timed-event saddle are in the height, weight, shape, length of the seat, the swells and the absence of any horn on the bronc saddle."

"What are swells?"

"Those are the side extensions on the front."

"There sure is a lot to these saddles and riggings."

He grinned. "Yep. There is."

She smiled back. "I'm learning so much."

"Glad you're enjoying this," he said. "And that I'm not boring you."

He could read me the back of a cereal box in that voice and not bore me.

"Far from it," she said, keeping her thoughts to herself. "I'm lucky to be here with a cowboy who knows all the things and can explain them to me."

"It's my pleasure, darlin'," he said. "See those stirrup leathers?"

She nodded.

"They're set well forward, and free swinging, so the bronc rider can place his spurs where needed for mark out and spurring."

He enjoyed explaining things to her and she enjoyed listening to him, and learning.

Both left the rodeo stadium happy after a great event.

* * *

On the way home from the rodeo, they went through the drive through at the local soft serve dairy place.

After waiting in the long line, she ordered a vanilla cone dipped in chocolate and he ordered a vanilla cone.

They would eat them as he drove home.

"That was a busy place," Emma said. "Is it usually that busy?"

"On rodeo weekends it is," he said. "And keep in mind that every person in that stadium is now heading out to go somewhere, so many of us stop for refreshing ice-cream."

They enjoyed talking over what they'd seen at the rodeo and eating their ice-cream cones as he drove. Soon they were in that long stretch between Cody and his home.

Usually there were few cars but today was an exception. Traffic was heavier because of the rodeo which had drawn people from all over.

Neither of them noticed the Hispanic man who'd recognized her in the stands when she'd taken the cowboy hat off.

He followed them onto the road to Cody and beyond, but as they turned off the main road onto the road which led to his home, the man had kept on driving instead of following them down it.

As soon as he reached his destination for the evening, he ordered a beer and then dialed a number. "Jefe, the señorita, I have seen her."

He listened. "Si. At the rodeo tonight. And then I followed."

The cartel had found her.

* * *

Destry and Emma arrived home and let Scout out to do his nightly patrol before turning in.

When Scout returned, Destry let him inside and then leaned in to kiss Emma softly on the lips.

They might be sharing his house, but as this was their official first date, Destry would treat it as such.

As his grandfather would have approved, he was courting the woman he was falling in love with. And that felt better than he would have ever imagined.

With a soft sigh, and a smile on those just kissed lips, Emma said, "Good night, Destry. I enjoyed this evening at the rodeo."

"I did too," he said. "Sweet dreams, Emma."

Emma went to bed and fell asleep, still thinking of their kiss and all that she'd seen at the rodeo.

Destry took much longer to fall asleep.

She was just down the hall sleeping and he wanted to do more than just kiss her. It required the discipline he applied to so many situations. Finally, he slept.

* * *

Destry woke instantly.

Emma, stood in the open doorway of his room

He must have heard her open the door.

She stood wearing a thin white nightgown with tiny pink flowers.

The picture of innocence.

Was she sleepwalking?

"Emma," he said her name softly.

When she didn't answer, he spoke again. "Emma, did you have another bad dream?"

"At first, but then it changed. Instead of the bad men coming to kill me, I dreamed I was right here, with you."

She took a shy step closer, into his room, her eyes sleepy but wide open.

Awake. Not sleepwalking. She'd intended to come in here.

"And then what happened?" he asked, smiling at her, intrigued and surprised she'd been dreaming about him.

He certainly dreamed about her often enough. Often enough to wake him and leave him wanting her.

"You kissed me again," she spoke with a quiet smile, as if remembering their kiss.

"Is that what you would like me to do now?"

Shyly, she nodded.

Destry rose from the bed, walked over to her, and then slid his hands around her and down to her hips.

He pulled her close to him and bent down to kiss her lips.

Her breathy little response and the way her breathing changed told him she wanted more than a kiss.

Slowly, ever so slowly, he gave her what she wanted, until she was naked in his arms. In his bed.

And as she gave herself to him, fully, he worshipped every bit of her body, by touch and by kiss.

It was the most tender way she had ever been touched, been kissed, been spoken to, and it made her feel like the most beautiful woman in the world.

This went beyond sex, beyond desire, beyond flesh, as soul to soul, they were finally one.

* * *

The next afternoon, shortly before sunset, Destry and Scout were walking in the pasture, checking the perimeter.

It had become their pattern since Emma had come to live with them.

Scout barked at something in the sky before Destry heard it or saw it.

He looked up to see what Scout was barking at, expecting to see a bird, though Scout didn't usually bark at birds.

A drone was flying above them. Likely the drone saw him, when he saw it, as it suddenly turned and headed away from him, in the direction it had probably come from.

His Delta instincts kicked in, telling him this was no accident. As far as he knew, none of his neighbors owned a drone. And he wasn't close enough to one of the ranches which used them to check on their cattle or horses for it to have strayed into his area.

Still, he picked up his cell phone to call his closest neighbor, Chuck to verify.

Dialing, he waited for the retired cowboy to answer.

"Destry, what's up?" Chuck said.

"A drone just flew over my head," Destry said. "You know anything about that?"

"Yeah, I saw it too, just a few minutes ago, then it headed over to your place. Thought maybe you got a new toy."

"Not mine," Destry said. "Never seen it before."

"Well, then you ought to know, I saw an unusual, strange car at the entrance to our road. Saw it pause, by the side of the road, before it ran on down the road in a hurry. I thought it strange at the time. I was coming home from the rodeo, driving behind all y'all about four trucks back."

Destry didn't believe in coincidences. Not this kind.

Most of the time, coincidences were manufactured by men, to attain something they wanted.

"Chuck, notify me immediately if you see or hear anything else out of the ordinary."

"Will do, and I'll ask the others to do the same."

"Thanks, man," Destry said. "I'm putting in a call to the sheriff next. They might come by."

"No problem," Chuck said. "You know your neighbors have got your six. We'll all keep an eye out. Keep me posted by text, day or night."

Chuck wore a hearing aide, and took it out at night, but he always had his cell phone on, and it would light up if someone messaged him or called.

"Will do," Destry said.

Both men hung up and then Destry walked to the house.

Pearl needed to be told, and he had to warn her to stay inside the house, where she wouldn't be spotted.

Hopefully she hadn't been already, but Destry knew it would be best to surmise that she might have been.

She just had to take off that cowboy hat at the rodeo. Dammit. She was concealed beneath it until then.

I only stepped away to get water bottles and came right back.

His gut told him that's when she'd been spotted. The moments when he'd stepped away.

He'd had a gut feeling the minute he saw her without the hat on, fanning herself.

A pretty woman like her would catch any man's eye and the fanning would increase that likelihood.

He hadn't been fast enough to reach her to tell her to put the hat back on.

Today there wasn't one damn reason for anyone to be flying a drone over his place.

If he'd had his rifle on him, he'd have shot the damn thing down immediately. No matter who was flying it.

"Good boy, Scout," he told his dog. "Come on. You've earned an extra treat."

Scout, who was already wagging his tail at being called a good boy, was by Destry's side now and woofed once. Then he was all about getting to the house for his treat.

Destry opened the back door and called out, "Pearl?"

She appeared around the corner with a dust rag in her

hand, her hair tied back in a pale blue bow, wearing a light blue, white, and pink sundress with a tiny floral pattern. She had her shoes off again and was now wearing pale pink polish on her toes.

Her face lit up when she smiled. "Yes, Destry?"

He caught his breath, unprepared for the sight of her.

If she wasn't the image of a domestic goddess, he didn't know who or what was.

The innocent beauty looking at him with that light in her eyes hit him with an emotional punch. He would protect her with his life, if needed.

Any man who touched her, or harmed a hair on her head, would die.

"Darlin'," he would be careful how he worded it. "We have a problem. Scout spotted a drone flying over my place, so I'm going to insist that you stay inside and away from the windows."

"Oh!" She gasped, putting her hand to her throat. "Do you think they saw me?"

"I don't know for sure, but it's best to say they did and take precautions."

He pulled his phone out as he went into the living room to close the drapes over the big picture window. "I'm calling the sheriff."

Curtains closed, he waited for the sheriff to pick up.

"Sheriff Colt here," he answered.

"Got a problem out here, Sheriff," Destry said. "A drone flew over my place less than ten minutes ago. My neighbor saw it too. Somebody's nosing around."

"I'm sending Deputy Brown your way now, and I'll call a meeting of the task force," Sheriff Colt said. "Best be on alert now and be prepared for anything."

"Already on that, Sheriff." Destry said, as he gave his dog a well-deserved treat. Then he hung up the phone.

Scout took his treat and went to lay down in the corner.

Destry turned to Pearl, who was sitting in a wing chair.

"Is the Sheriff coming?" she asked.

"Deputy Brown is on his way," he said.

"Oh, I liked him," Pearl said, with a soft smile.

She was clearly scared, but trying not to show it.

He would have pulled her into his arms to reassure her. But he didn't have time right now.

"I'm going to put Arrow in the barn," he said.

"Okay," she nodded.

"Once he's got feed and water, I'll be back in."

She just nodded again.

"If you need Scout, just call for him."

She didn't have a cell phone. Hadn't needed one.

"I won't be gone long," he said. Then he went out the door.

Arrow came over to him, once he opened the barn door. The usual routine, open the door, fetch hay, and water. Arrow knew it by heart and was always ready to be fed.

Once Destry squared away his horse, he headed back to the house to check on Pearl and to get his guns ready.

If the cartel was coming here, he would need every gun and each piece of ammunition he had at hand.

Who knew how many men the cartel would send?

Could be quite a few.

Chapter Eleven

Inside the house, Pearl still sat quietly on the chair, which was in the corner, away from the window, staring at the floor with a scared look on her face.

He went over to her. "You're going to be safe, darlin', he said as he took her hands and pulled her to her feet. "Come here."

She stepped close to him.

He wrapped his arms around her, holding her close, feeling how she silently shook. Giving her a squeeze he said, "Breathe, sweetheart, just breathe."

She took a few shaky breaths which seemed to calm her some.

"You can help me," he said. "Come on."

That got her attention, and she popped her head up and stepped back, watching him.

He took her by the hand and walked with her into his bedroom. Inside, he opened the full walk-in closet.

At the sight of it, she gasped.

One whole wall on the right side was guns and knives.

"As you can see, I'm more than somewhat prepared," he

said. "Now you can help me load them with ammo. I'll show you how."

Her eyes still wide, she said, "Okay." Then she took a breath and let it out. "I don't know how to load a gun."

"I'll start you on the revolvers," he said. He pulled two guns down. Picking up a big box of ammo he carried it all over to the bed and set them on top.

Patting the bed, he gave her a look that said sit here.

She sat where he'd indicated.

"Okay," he picked up one of the revolvers, opened it and said, "With these revolvers, you drop the bullets in each of the holes one at a time."

Then he showed her how to drop a bullet in and handed her the gun.

She sat looking at it in her hand. "I've never held a gun before," she said.

"It's okay," he said. "I'm teaching you."

"Is it going to go off?" she asked.

"No, darlin' it's not, unless you pull the trigger."

"Oh, okay."

"Load those two for me and then lay them on the bed. I've got other guns to load."

"Okay." She began to drop a bullet in.

He reached the closet again and began loading the big guns. Two AR 15's and an AK.

She paused in her task to watch him, and her jaw dropped as he loaded them all so fast.

His movements were smooth, practiced, and then done. He turned to look at her.

Now she was seeing the soldier, the Delta Force opera-tive, in his element, and he was far from the gentle nurse, and the strong cowboy she'd come to know. But equally Destry. In all three roles he was all Destry.

Destry, the man, was capable in all three arenas. A man who got things done.

He was the sexiest man she'd ever seen.

She wondered if there was anything he couldn't do.

And those eyes, in that handsome face, determined to keep her safe, caring about her, carried an intensity that called to her soul.

She was falling hard, head over heels in love.

And she might not see tomorrow.

She glanced down at the two guns, not wanting to think about that, and made sure all the chambers were full.

"I think I'm done with these," she said.

He was to her side quickly. "Good job," he said, and then he closed the chambers and put the safeties on.

Next, he loaded some nine millimeters.

"You have a lot of guns," she said.

"I enjoy collecting them and shooting them," he said.

"How often do you shoot them?"

"I used to shoot daily," he said. "Practicing was part of my job. Now I shoot a couple times a week depending on my work schedule at the Clinic."

"Where do you shoot them? Here on your ranch?"

"No. There's the occasional coyote, but I don't have livestock to worry about yet. So they don't come here looking for a meal. And Scout is here always marking his territory."

"So that's why he does that."

"Yep." He was done loading all his guns and pulled out his phone. "Calling gram," he said.

"Hello, dear boy," she said.

"Gram, I need you to tell everyone to stay away from my place," he said. "Except Jake. Put him on."

"My goodness, Destry, is everything all right over there?"

"Yes, but maybe not for long. Get Jake."

He never spoke to his gram that way, but the clock was ticking, and he needed Jake here now.

Jake picked up. "Situation?"

"Yep," Destry said. "Need backup. Come in quiet."

"Roger that," Jake said and hung up.

Destry heard a car coming up the road. He moved to the living room and peered out the window.

A sheriff's car was rolling up the road, taking its time, no lights or siren.

Perfect. If they were coming for her, the team coming in to defend needed to come in quiet and not raise attention. Hopefully the drone had reported back and wasn't still up there, flying around.

If he saw it up there again, he would shoot it.

He slung the AR over his shoulder and then caught Emma staring at him with wide eyes.

"Deputy Brown is coming," he said. "He's going to stay in the house with you, while I circle my property to see if anything unusual is out there."

"Like another drone?"

He nodded. "Like another drone. I'll wait till he's inside with you."

"Thank you," she said.

He could tell she was scared, and he didn't blame her.

She'd already been through one shooting and survived. That was enough for one lifetime. If he could spare her another, he would.

Deputy Brown pulled up by the garage and Destry stepped outside. "Go ahead and park her in the barn," he called.

Not that a sheriff's car would stop any cartel member,

but they didn't need to broadcast who was here to help him defend Pearl.

Once the deputy parked the car inside, he headed for the house. Destry opened the door and let him in.

Pearl was standing in the kitchen now, away from the sink, with a strange expression on her face.

"Ma'am," Deputy Brown nodded to her.

"Thank you for coming," she said in a soft voice.

Destry touched her elbow. "You're going to be okay," he said.

"I'm, I'm afraid to go near the sink," she said. "It has a window."

So, it did. And no curtains, just the way Destry liked it. The back of the house didn't need curtains, there were no neighbors to see in.

"Are you thirsty?" he asked.

She nodded. "I just wanted some water," she said. "My mouth is so dry."

"Nerves," Deputy Brown said. "Happens to my sister too. I'll fetch you a glass."

"Heading to the barn and for a look about," Destry said.

Deputy Brown was already running water into a glass for her. "Go on," he said. "I'll look after Pearl."

Destry gave a nod and headed out, taking Scout with him.

Scout was faster and a better patroller than he was.

In the barn, he closed the door so the deputy's car wouldn't show.

Then he walked over and opened the door to the tack room went inside and walked over to a large rough box against the wall that opened to another gun safe.

He put in the combination and opened the safe. More rifles and a few grenades sat inside. He pulled everything out and carried it back to the house before heading back out with Scout to look around.

There were no footprints and no signs of another drone anywhere.

Destry was headed back to the house from the west side of his property when he sensed the presence of someone nearby.

"Cuz," he heard Jake's voice so low he almost missed it. "I haven't seen anyone out here. Where's your woman?"

"Back at the house with the deputy," Destry said.

"You trust him?" Jake asked.

"He's already saved her life once and he's DEA task force, so yes. Otherwise, I would've said no."

"All right. I'm headed to the barn," Jake said, handing Destry a handheld radio. "Don't tell anyone I'm here."

Destry nodded and went back to the house.

* * *

Sheriff Colt called James Arnold, the SAC of the DEA task force, who then set up a task force meeting of the men available.

They met at a small park outside of Billings on the way to Cody, not far from Destry's ranch.

Sheriff Colt, DEA's James Arnold, Deputy Morris Cooper, DEA Eldon Marks, DEA Scott Baker, and Billings police officer Levi Parker gathered around in a circle to talk.

"Just so we know who we're dealing with," the DEA analyst said. "Pearl Hayes is a recently assumed name. Her real name is Emma Pearl Smith, and she was the secretary for Clement Oakley Esquire who was recently killed by the Sinaloa cartel. He'd represented two cartel men and botched what would have been a money laundering scheme. Money got wired to the wrong account, their boss accused him of stealing it and put out the hit."

"Her missing persons info has been out there for a while," detective Austin Foster said. "But I've never seen her, so I didn't put two and two together."

"Oakley, her boss, set her up with a plane ticket to Bozeman and got her out of town before the hit," Brett Collier said. "So, he must've known trouble was coming. He also set up Nathan Smalls to take her to a condo he owns in Bozeman."

"Smalls isn't a criminal, but he's street smart. Grew up in New York. Was a professional boxer. Now he's a bouncer, teaches boxing on the side when he's in the mood and takes on the occasional side job. Looks like the lawyer got Mr. Smalls out of some legal trouble, the boxer owed him a favor, and Oakley called it in."

"She tried calling her boss once and then her phone went to a dead end. No record of any calls after that. I'm guessing Smalls found out Oakley was dead and then the two of them went on the run. He would've known not to take her to that condo. It's easy to find out Oakley owned the condo. In Bozeman, she mailed her I.D.s to her parents and became Pearl Hayes. They were heading to Billings when they were shot at by the cartel."

"The cartel must think she knows something or has something, so they came after her. He'd been in his office deleting records when he was killed. They tore his office apart looking for something. But they weren't computer geeks, or they would've found there was a download from Oakley's computer onto a flash drive. Accounting records. A list of names and phone numbers. She might have those records, she might not."

"I don't think she's done anything wrong. She's likely an

innocent party, but they don't see it that way. And her boss didn't help matters, by giving her that plane ticket to Montana. Made it look like she has something to hide."

"Well, we've got a situation now," Sheriff Colt aid. "Destry called to say he spotted a drone flying around his place and his neighbor saw a man in a truck hanging around the road coming in. Sounds like they've found her."

"How the hell did they find her?" James Arnold growled. "Hell, you wouldn't even tell me where you hid her."

"That's right," Sheriff Colt said, "And so far, she's still alive."

* * *

The night sky was dark, and there were no streetlights or businesses on this stretch of land. Even the few new houses that had been built recently weren't lit at night.

Jake and Destry both had night vision goggles. The task force members wore them as well. The only one who didn't have them was Emma, and she was hiding.

Jake had set up in the barn and turned off the one large light Destry had mounted on the front of the barn.

Inside the house, the drapes were all pulled, and the lights were off.

Emma was hiding in Destry's walk in closet, where he usually stored his guns.

In the far corner of the closet, where he'd pushed an old trunk, she'd curled up next to it, hugging herself. He'd draped a quilt over her and the trunk. If she stayed still, she might go unnoticed.

He didn't think any of the cartel members would get that far, but he wasn't taking chances.

And she wasn't alone.

Scout lay on the floor of the closet, facing the door, listening and guarding her.

Once he was told to guard, that's what he would do.

From where Emma was hidden at first, she only heard silence and then she heard Scout panting and knew he was still there, guarding the door.

The men were in position, waiting, and her nerves were so on edge she started to shake. She whimpered.

And then Scout was there, by her side, his nose burrowing under the quilt, until she felt his cold doggie nose against her cheek, followed by a wet doggie kiss.

"Oh, Scout, you're such a good boy," she whispered. "Thank you. I love you too."

Something about his presence had settled her heartbeat back down to normal, and the threat of hyperventilating passed.

Scout went back to his earlier guard position and laid down again, to wait.

Then the silence was broken by a burst of gunfire.

Who started shooting, she didn't know. But whichever side had started it, it was answered.

Gunfire now had to be coming from both sides.

It sounded like it was coming from different directions, from everywhere.

Not knowing exactly what was going on was driving her crazy, and she had to fight the urge to go out and look.

She wouldn't, but she wanted to.

Loud. It was so loud.

She'd known it would be, it wasn't the first gunfight she'd been near, but that didn't prepare her for the audible assault on her ears and the fear it caused. The memories it brought back.

Nothing could have prepared her for that.

She bowed her head and covered her ears as the sounds took her back to the shooting on the highway and the gunmen.

They were back.

They were going to kill her.

A cold sweat broke out on her neck and the sounds changed as if they were coming from far away. As if she were moving. But she was still.

She began to rock back and forth, holding in her sobs, self-preservation amid her flashback.

They were coming.

It was like in her bad dreams but for real as the nightmares mixed with the reality.

Then suddenly it all stopped.

So captured by the flashback, she didn't realize at first that the shooting had stopped.

That the closet door had opened.

Then Scout was there, again, kissing her arm when he couldn't reach her cheek this time. Pulling her back.

And then that voice again.

Pulling her. Calling her name.

The man who had comforted her before, the man whose voice was pulling her back into the now, away from the past, was here.

"Emma, baby, you're all right now." His arms scooped under her, and lifted her, as he kept talking. "They're all dead. It's safe, baby. No one is going to hurt you."

He carried her out of the closet and into his room, then sat on the bed, cradling her as her sobs began to leak out.

Tears flooded her eyes and down, soaking his shirt, as he held her and rocked her.

"Shh," he murmured into her hair. "I've got you, babe. I've got you now. You're safe."

When she finally stopped, she was still and silent for a moment as he continued to rock her. She sensed that he would rock her for as long as she needed.

But now, she needed to see him, so she raised her head to look at him with wet eyelashes and a tear-streaked face.

"I'm safe," she repeated, looking into his eyes.

His gaze, calm and steady, looking back at her told her that she was.

"Yes," he said. "You're safe."

She threaded her arms around his neck and held on as if something would take her away. "Thank you."

"Sweetheart, you don't need to thank me," he said as he squeezed her back. "You never need to thank me."

"But I want to," she said. "Because my heart feels it."

He kissed her forehead and then leaned back again to continue searching her eyes. "How are you feeling?"

"Shaky, but not scared shaky," she said. "More like drained of energy."

"Exhausted," he said.

She nodded.

He knew. He really knew.

"I need to go back out there to talk to the team," he said. "And they'll all want to know that you're okay. You can rest here, with Scout."

"No, I want to go with you," she said. "I want to stay with you. And Scout will need to go out."

Destry looked over to where Scout was standing by the door quietly waiting.

Ordinarily he would have woofed.

Emma was right.

"Are you ready?" he asked.

When she nodded, he stood, still holding her.

"You can put me down," she said. "I won't crumble now."

"Never thought you would," he said.

That confidence in her, back in his voice, reassured her as it always did.

Around him, she felt that that she could do anything.

Chapter Twelve

rrangements were being made for Emma to go into protective custody. They would be here for her soon.

Destry had talked to the team about her, emphasizing the importance of medical care for her shoulder, and counseling to help her with the nightmares.

She might no longer be under his care, but he still cared for her. He cared deeply.

They were supposed to say goodbye.

He was supposed to let her go.

He kept his feelings to himself, but his mind was working, the angles, the ways they might stay connected.

Life could turn on a dime, and he wanted her to be able to reach him if she needed him.

"Emma," he gestured for her to follow him, and went into grams bedroom.

She followed him in, and he closed the door.

"Memorize this," Destry said, holding a white piece of paper with a phone number written on it in black ink.

Emma looked at the paper and repeated the number to herself.

"They'll make you change phones, might give you burner phones, but my number won't change, and you can call it any time of day or night."

"I thought I'm not supposed to contact anyone from my past, not even my family."

"Right," he said. "Memorize that number anyway."

"Okay," she said. She went to take the paper, but he put his hand over hers, stopping her.

"You didn't get this from me," he said. "And you won't write it down anywhere. You'll have to remember it."

"I'll remember it." She repeated the number, speaking low, and then nodded.

He squeezed her hand and then let go.

She swallowed and then looked up at him. "Where do you think they'll take me?"

"I have no idea," he said. "And if I knew, and they found out I knew, they'd move you. But know this. If you need me, I will come. Wherever you are."

Their gazes locked and held, tears beginning to brim in hers, intensity in his.

He ran his thumb across her lips, his touch making them tingle. Never taking his gaze from hers, he lowered his lips until he kissed her.

The kiss was filled with love and a promise. She didn't want it to end.

They were meant to be together. They both knew it.

Even though circumstances were getting in the way.

His words, as he pulled away slightly, sunk into her soul. His arms still around her waist, keeping her close.

He looked down into her eyes and said, "Wherever you are, darlin,' I *will* find you."

Tears glistened in her eyes. "I don't want to leave you."

"I know," he said. "But I need you to go, for now. I need you to be safe. If not for you, then for me."

She nodded. She had no other choice right now that would keep them both safe. She didn't want to endanger him. Wouldn't endanger him. And she already had.

He might be special ops trained, and very good at it, but he was only human. His training didn't make him invincible. And she would not be the cause of him not coming home one day.

"I'll go," she said. "I know it's the best choice to keep us both safe."

He squeezed her close and kissed her forehead.

She closed her eyes. "Don't forget me," she whispered.

"Won't happen," he said. "Couldn't if I tried." He placed his finger beneath her chin and tilted it up, then bent to kiss her again.

This kiss was so deep, so sweeping that there was no doubt she could ever forget it and him. And his kiss was telling her that he wouldn't forget it and her either.

It was a kiss to last a lifetime.

Keeping her eyes closed she soaked in every sensation, every second.

When they came up for air, and he slowly pulled away, she held the feelings around her and within her, so that she would never lose them. Would carry them with her forever.

He traced her face with his fingers as if he would memorize her, his gaze telling her she was beautiful to him.

"We'll have to go back out," he said. "They'll be here for you soon."

She gave a deep sigh. "I know."

He threaded his fingers through hers and walked her back out into the hallway.

"I'll miss you, and Scout, and Arrow, and this place," she said. "It's peaceful here."

"Most of the time it is," he said with a smile.

"When bad guys aren't trying to kill me." She smiled back, trying to lighten things for him, the way he was always lightening things for her.

She didn't know if she was succeeding.

Then they had arrived to get her and too soon she was climbing into the car with the shaded windows.

As the car drove away, she turned to watch through a darkened window.

The ranch, the man, and the dog, grew smaller as she sent up a prayer and a vow.

Someday, I will return. Please God, make it so.

Destry watched the car roll away slowly down the gravel drive, taking her away from him.

Though he wouldn't say the words to her, nor voice them to another, as he watched her go, he determined that one day, once he'd finally determined that she would be safe here, he would bring her back to him.

He would bring her home.

Scout came up to him and woofed.

Destry reached down to scratch his head. "Yes, boy, she will be back one day, and we'll be right here waiting for her."

Scout woofed once more in agreement and then he nudged Destry's leg with a frisbee after Destry had stood too long watching the car which was no longer in his sight.

"All right, boy." He reached for the frisbee, and then threw it and watched his dog racing after it, like the wind.

Epilogue

Brett Collier came up with a plan and the FBI guy helped him to plan and then put it into place.

They had the suitcase.

The thumb drive had been replaced in the suitcase after copying the information.

Then the suitcase was hidden in the lawyer's condo, which the cartel hadn't checked out when they were chasing Emma. A "tip" made its way to the cartel that the lawyer had sent Mr. Smalls to the condo with a suitcase. It couldn't hurt Mr. Smalls who was dead now.

The condo was watched.

They knew exactly when the suitcase had been picked up by a cartel affiliate.

The cartel now knew where their money was, though they still couldn't get their hands on it. They knew Emma didn't have it. Or the fob. They had the suitcase and the fob.

Emma didn't have anything they wanted, but going after Emma had been a costly mistake when it came to manpower. Twice they'd failed to kill or capture her, and she had been defended by DEA agents each time.

Brett Collier believed the cartel would see that as poor ROI.

He said even criminal organizations with vengeful men at the top might look at a cost benefit to their actions. What did it cost and how much money would it make them?

Even still, they waited a few more months to be sure the interest in Emma had died down.

Finally Brett paid Emma a visit.

She was now going by the name Barbara Scott and living in Reno, Nevada where she worked at an office supply company, in their back office, scheduling shipments.

Her head bent down, attentive to her work, she didn't notice the two men standing just outside her office door.

Brett rapped on the door frame with his hand, two times.

Startled, she straightened and turned.

"Brett, what are you doing here?" she asked.

"Brought someone to see you," he said, and then he stepped aside to let the man behind him step up.

The man who visited her in her dreams filled the doorway as he stepped into the room.

She gasped.

Destry.

"Are you ready to come home?" he said.

She nearly flew into his arms, she moved so fast, and then he was holding her, and she was holding on so tight.

Like she never wanted to let go.

"Yes," she breathed out and then she looked up into his eyes. "I want to go home."

And at that moment, held within his arms, she knew that she already was.

THE END

Sample, Chapter One: To Catch an Elf: Pennsylvania Fighter Pilot

Zeke Kingsley and Beverly Westwood were holding hands in Upstate New York, strolling past quaint little shops that bored him to death, when he spotted an antique Christmas elf sitting behind a store window, staring out at him.

The elf wore red-and-white striped pants with a green vest covered with stars, along with a red belt with a gold buckle. A red-and-white striped hat with tiny bells sat atop her long blonde hair in braids. Her long legs and arms were bendable for posing. Pointed green shoes with bells finished her outfit.

She was unique, unlike any Christmas elf that Zeke had ever seen.

People all over the country would post pictures of their elves on the Biggest Busy Elf Contest website.

All to try to win a five-thousand-dollar prize. Beverly had decided to enter the contest and she wanted to win.

That elf is perfect.

He almost laughed out loud as he stopped suddenly.

When Zeke didn't step forward with her, but stopped

and tugged her back toward him, Beverly turned with a frown.

"I've found you the perfect elf, for your elf contest," he said. Then he pointed to it.

Her frown deepened as she looked at the doll.

"It's unique," he said. "No one else will have one like it. Let's go in."

"No." Beverly adamantly shook her head. "Antique shops are dreadful, stinky stores full of old things that smell." She crinkled her perfect nose, and adjusted her fur coat around her shoulders, as if she were suddenly chilled.

Which made no sense, as it was a warm fall evening and would not begin to cool off for another hour.

He watched her, thinking.

Had to be her reaction to the store, or to the elf. Interesting.

His high-society girlfriend was suddenly showing cracks in her normal façade for the first time since he'd known her.

Everyone had a face they presented to the world, and one they used in the dark, when no one else was around. That had been his early discovery as a child, watching grownups, and his adult life in college and beyond hadn't shown him anything different.

I wonder what caused her extreme dislike of antique shops and the old things they display. She likely wouldn't enjoy historical museums either.

"Never mind," he said. "If you're cold, we can stop for a cappuccino instead."

"That sounds much better," Beverly said, her usual mask back in place.

With her perfect nose, porcelain skin, cool blue eyes, and platinum blonde hair, she could have stepped out of a fashion magazine.

And she knew it.

That, and her family money, gave her a haughty air at times.

Beverly also loved to show off her double D breasts that her family's old money had bought her. They always caught men's attention, and she loved the attention.

She flashed him a smile, one that would have had most men catering to her every whim.

It never worked on him.

The first time she'd tried it, he'd simply stood there watching her, for what most would have considered a very long time, before giving her a wink, to let her know he was onto her and unmoved by her charms.

Then he had walked away.

That made him as attractive as hell to her, as he knew it would.

He knew a thing or two about inheriting money and had kept his inheritance quiet, refusing to let anyone know how much he had, but implying that he had "enough." So, he could easily behave as if he did not care about her family money, or their influence.

Though, in truth, he believed that having more was always better. The more you had, the more you could do things that you otherwise couldn't.

He also had a knack for watching people, and learning things about them that they might not even have known themselves.

She saw him as strong in mind and character.

Beverly was right.

Never would he let another woman control him or emasculate him. He'd learned strength, growing up with a mother who controlled everything. Growing up without a father, he'd had no other choice as a child.

Just as his mother had shown one face to the world, and another to him at home, he too learned to present a mask.

The difference was, he never let his slip and never lost his temper. He was always in control of himself.

Beverly knew nothing of his past.

He'd told her that both of his parents were dead, and she'd dropped the subject at once, not wanting to hear of unpleasant things.

She tried to avoid hearing unpleasant things.

It did bring a degree of sympathy into her eyes after that, and if the subject came up, she would steer people away from it, as if she was doing him a kindness.

He really didn't care about that. He found watching her amusing.

She had no clue how much he watched her. Watching women was something he enjoyed.

They went on to have cappuccinos, and then to finish her early Christmas shopping.

October seemed early to him, but people did shop that early. He was more of a shop the night before kind of man and would pick from whatever was left in the stores to choose from.

To him, Christmas was no big deal. Other people didn't celebrate Christmas the way he would have.

Santa rarely brought him something he wanted.

This Christmas would be different.

* * *

Later, when Zeke was back at work in Manhattan, he called the antique shop and described the elf.

"Do you still have the elf?" he asked.

"Yes, we still have it," the woman answered.

"Excellent," he said. "I'll purchase the elf, if you can send it out to be cleaned and to be filled with new stuffing."

"But that would decrease the value of the antique," the shop owner protested.

"True, but then I can gift it to my fiancée, who has terrible allergies. This is a Christmas gift, and I don't want it to make her sick. She will love the gift, but not if it has old stuffing. It must be hypoallergenic stuffing for her, all the way."

"Oh, I see," the woman said, though she was still clearly distressed at the idea of devaluing the antique.

He could tell by her tone, and by the fact that she had yet to agree to it.

"The elf is old and comes with a history," she said. "Her name is Tananna. The girl who owned her died and her mother took the doll and packed it away in a trunk, where it stayed until everything in the house was sold in an estate sale many years later. We've tried to find others like her, but there seem to be none. She is unique and should be preserved."

"I'm not going to change what she looks like. Just her stuffing. Can it be done? I will pay extra," he said.

Throwing more money at something often brought the result you wanted.

"Yes, it can be done," she said with a sigh, giving in. "I know people who restore dolls."

Zeke gave her his credit card number, and the purchase was made.

He would surprise Beverly with the elf, just before December and the start of the online elf contest.

They'd be spending the Christmas holiday in Miami, Florida.

Beverly would need a dog-sitter, and house-sitter for her

house in the Large Bass Lake subdivision in the Pocono Mountains.

A house she never went to unless she wanted to ski all weekend. Which she only did once a year now that the newness had worn off. Once the newness wore off anything, she was done with it.

He knew all about newness wearing off. But he had the perfect house-sitter for her, one who house sat for his cousin not long ago.

A blonde named Marcie, with curves and a sweet smile, who also loved dogs.

She was perfect.

* * *

After the elf arrived, he looked the doll over. You could see the recent stitching, where they'd cut the back of the fabric of the doll and then stitched it back together There was plenty of new stuffing.

Good.

Taking scissors, he ripped open the stitching, careful not to cut anything that would leave a mark.

Then he pulled out just enough stuffing and inserted a camera inside. Threading the thin part, that would sit behind the eye of the doll up into her face, behind the eye, he fiddled with it until everything was in place. Then made sure the stuffing hid everything, so you could not feel the equipment.

After that, he restitched the doll. It took a while, because no one had taught him how to sew, but eventually he got it done.

Finished, he looked the doll over.

No one will know.

He would give Beverly the doll tomorrow night.

* * *

Beverly still didn't like the elf much. Even though the doll now smelled fresh and new and had been cleaned.

"What is this?" She leaned back against his leather couch, away from the doll. "Why would you buy this old thing for me?"

"I bought her for you, so you can win," he spoke as if it should be obvious. "This elf is unique, no one else will have one like it. The owner of the shop tried to locate another one like it and had no luck, so this must be the only one in existence. The other contestants will be buying new elves off the shelves. I know how you can't stand to see any woman wearing the same dress as you, so I don't believe you'd want your elf to look like everyone else's. Look, I even had her cleaned and re-stuffed for you, so there's no bad smell."

His tone implied that he'd gone to a lot of trouble for her.

She appeared confused.

"Her insides are all new?" she asked, though he'd just told her that they were.

Patient, he nodded.

"Well," she hesitated, picking the doll up and giving it a quick sniff, to double-check.

He knew it didn't smell bad.

"Thank you," she finally said. "I do want to win the contest."

She sat the doll back down on the coffee table and stared at it for a long time.

Finally, she spoke. "It's looking at me."

"Most dolls do," he said. "And you've been staring at it for a while. Don't make yourself paranoid over a silly doll."

"Well, I'm not taking this elf to Miami with us," she said. "I don't want to have to look at her, or have her looking at me, every time we come back to our room."

"You don't have to take the elf to Miami," he said. "Let the house-sitter take the pictures for the contest and send them to you. It's not like she'll have anything else to do, besides walking the dog once a day."

Ginger, Beverly's little King Charles Spaniel, was easy to take care of, this was true. She just needed to be fed, watered, and walked. Which was all Beverly did with her. The rest of the time Ginger was at doggie daycare. But they didn't board dogs overnight.

"That's a great idea," Beverly said. "Didn't you say you knew someone?"

"Yes," he said. "My cousin hired a house-sitter a few months ago, and she was good. I'll call him for her contact number and take care of it. And, if you don't want to take the elf home with you tonight, she can stay here until you hand her off to the sitter."

He didn't tell her the house-sitter's name was Marcie Hayes, or that he'd had Marcie's number for months. He'd even had Marcie investigated. He knew a lot about Marcie Hayes that his girlfriend didn't need to know.

She didn't need to know a lot of things. Luckily, she was too busy being pretty to be more inquisitive.

Beverly gave him a beautiful smile, and then leaned forward and kissed him.

His smile after that kiss was deep.

Not merely because of the kiss.

He was visualizing Marcie with her soft curves, big blue eyes, and long blonde hair. She was pretty enough to be a doll herself. Pretty enough to be in pictures with the elf.

The elf would keep her company all through December, as she took pictures with it, for the elf contest.

And he would be watching.

It was the perfect plan.

* * *

Day one: Take a picture of you meeting the elf ...

The strangest request Marcie Hayes had received since she'd started her 'Home Sweet Home Sitting' house-sitting business, five years ago, sat on the kitchen table staring at her.

She stared back.

Ginger, the little dog she would be dog-sitting, had been barking since she'd walked in the front door, but she was supposed to read this note first, even before letting the dog out.

An antique Christmas elf sat on the table beside the note.

To be honest, Marcie found the Christmas elf more than a little creepy, with its weird eyes, and she thought, not for the first time since walking into the room, that its eyes were following her.

But doll eyes didn't follow people because dolls weren't alive. So, she brushed her initial thoughts aside.

Christmas elves of the stuffed variety, which had become popular, were supposed to be Santa's helpers, reporting back to Santa on whether a child had been good or not.

Though this antique elf didn't look the same as those

elves and did not look like an elf anyone should ever give a child, it was still a Christmas elf.

People all over the country would post pictures of their elves on the Biggest Busy Elf Contest website.

All to try to win the five-thousand-dollar prize. And Beverly wanted to win.

Marcie glanced down again at the instructions Beverly Westwood had left for her on the table in front of the elf. Picking up the paper she reread the part about the elf.

Meet Tananna, my Christmas elf. Isn't she wonderful? I'll bet no one has an elf just like her. She's an antique from one of those Slav countries. Czechoslovakia, or Poland, or Croatia, or something.

Marcie shook her head and thought: *She's covering such a wide range of Slav countries; she has no idea where it's from.* Marcie went back to reading the note.

I want to win the Biggest Busy Elf Contest, so this is very important. I want you to take a picture of my elf every day and text it to me. The grand prize this year is five thousand dollars! The pictures you take must be good. No blurry or off-centered ones.

I want one taken in each room of the house (so make sure it stays clean) doing Christmas stuff. I will tell you exactly what to do, so it will be easy.

We can do this! We can win! Here is the schedule:

Day one: Take a pic of you meeting the elf in the kitchen.

Day two: The elf watching you make breakfast. Make it a big breakfast. Bacon, fried eggs, toast, and hash-browns. Remember, everyone will see the picture! Position her so she is watching the pans on the stove while you cook, but not close enough that the elf might catch fire. Remember, she is old and is a valuable antique.

Marcie had to put the note back down on the table,

and step away as her emotions charged up. "She's telling me what to eat!" She voiced her opinion to the empty kitchen.

The little King Charles Spaniel started barking even more.

She needed to hurry through this note and let the dog out.

"I never eat a big breakfast!"

More barking answered her.

Usually, she just had a simple bowl of cereal or oatmeal.

"Now I must cook a big, greasy breakfast?" she muttered to herself. "I don't think so."

She paced and thought.

Beverly must be a control freak.

Only a control freak would tell someone else what to do, even down to what they had to eat. Only a control freak would attempt to control what was going on when they weren't around.

"I am not letting someone else tell me what to eat or drink. It's my body. I alone have the say in what goes into it."

Barking, barking, barking answered her.

She went back to the table and read the rest of the note.

Day three: Take a picture of the elf helping you put up the Christmas tree. The tree and decorations are all in the basement, clearly marked with which ones to use this year.

"Good gravy," Marcie said. "This woman is something else." She read faster.

Day four: Watch a Christmas DVD with the elf, in the living room. Watch the Rudolph movie for this picture. Make popcorn and use the Santa bowl.

Day five: Take a picture of the elf on the desk with the phone, reporting to Santa.

Day six: Take a picture of the elf on the bookshelf in the downstairs office/study picking out a Christmas story to read.

Day seven: Take a picture of the elf having hot cocoa. Then show her climbing up the tree because she's had too much sugar. Make sure no bulbs get broken. That is taking the naughty elf too far.

"I know who's taking things too far," Marcie muttered, ignoring the barking dog, which was starting to upset her, as usually she did not ignore people's dogs. She hurried to get through reading the message to the end.

Day eight: Take a picture of you and the elf, in the kitchen, baking Christmas cookies. The sugar cut-out kind. I want the kind you make from scratch, not the slice-and-bake ones, and no store-bought ready-made! There needs to be flour on the table, and the elf with the rolling pin.

"She doesn't even know if I can bake or cook. Nothing about food, or diet, or cooking was mentioned to me when I took this job." Marcie shook her head. "Unreal." She continued to read.

Day nine: Naughty elf takes a bite out of one of the cookies. Take a picture of the elf, and the rest of the cookie.

Day ten: Take a picture of the elf writing a letter to Santa.

"I know what I'd like to write to Santa about," Marcie said.

Day eleven: Take a picture of the elf upstairs in bed with you, reading a bedtime Christmas story. Be sure to wear cute pajamas.

"Now she's telling me what to wear," Marcie muttered. "I never agreed to be in pictures posted online, in bed, wearing cute pajamas. I don't even wear pajamas."

The white silk nightie she wore, which was her soft comfort sleep item and traveled with her, was not something she was willing to wear in pictures spread over the internet. Too much of her showed through it. But it was the softest, silkiest thing she had ever owned and sleeping in it was a way of pampering herself, something she needed when staying in other people's bedrooms.

"We're going to have to talk about this," Marcie said. "First, she isn't paying me enough to do all this, and second, I'm not wearing what she says, or eating what she says."

Marcie noted there was no offer to pay for all the food she was supposed to cook, or to pay for pajamas to appear in. Not that she was doing any of that stuff anyway. But, if she were inclined, it would not be coming out of her pay.

She went back to reading the list.

Day twelve: Take a bubble bath with the elf and set her on the shelf at the end of the tub where she won't really get wet. Just put some bubbles on her.

In disgust, Marcie stopped reading the list.

"So, I'm dog-sitting, house-sitting, and baby-sitting an elf doll, while the owner tells me what to eat and wear, and she wants me to take a bubble bath ... with an elf."

She hook her head. "This is crazy. And *none* of this was part of our original agreement. She owns the house and its contents and the dog. She does not own me. I provide a service she has paid for, which is not the same thing at all."

She skimmed down to the bottom of the elf pictures list, from day twelve on, and then read the final entries.

Day twenty-three: The day before Christmas Eve, the contest is over.

Day twenty-four: Christmas Eve, be ready to take a picture of the elf with the winning email when we win!

I know we have an edge because my elf is a very special antique elf. She doesn't stink like other antiques because she's been cleaned and restored, and even has new stuffing.

You won't see another elf like her on the internet, or anywhere else.

Not sure where Zeke found her, but she's the best gift ever.

I want you to think of her as your new best friend. She'll do everything with you this season, so you won't be alone, and you'll also have Ginger.

Ginger may bark at her, but she's just being silly.

Use your imagination and have lots of fun with the contest! The more pictures the better, that way I'll have plenty to choose from.

And you will receive a fifty-dollar bonus if we win!

No wonder Beverly wanted to try to cash in on the prize. But she wanted Marcie to do all the work. And she hadn't offered Marcie any portion of that good prize if they won.

Just a fifty-dollar bonus.

Fifty dollars wouldn't even cover all the groceries and other stuff she'd have to buy to meet all of Beverly's demands.

The only thing Beverly had to do was upload the pictures using her code into the form on the website. Her pictures would all be grouped together somehow by using that code.

Marcie would have to take the elf pictures and then send them to Beverly in Miami, where she was on holiday with her boyfriend, Zeke.

She'd gotten the job, because of Zeke, though she barely remembered meeting him, before she got in her car to leave a house-sitting job for his cousin.

The cousins had arrived at the homeowner's house together, after a trip.

She may not have remembered him, but he had remembered her.

Zeke had suggested her to his girlfriend, Beverly, when she'd needed a house-sitter and a dog-sitter.

Now here Marcie was, house-sitting a house in the Large Bass Lake subdivision in the Poconos, in December, and dog-sitting a King Charles Spaniel named Ginger, along with a creepy elf named Tananna.

Well, best to get on with it.

She moved the irritating note out of the way, pulled out her cell phone and selfie stick to take a picture and frowned. Then she stood next to the elf, forced a smile, and took the first photo on the list.

She texted it to Beverly.

The things I do for my clients. Sigh. Is this going to raise my phone bill?

I'm only going to send her one picture a day. Take as many as I want? I don't want to take any. So, unless I get a pay increase, one will have to do.

Opening the refrigerator, on the way out of the kitchen, before going to let Ginger out, she found bottled water, condiments, and a tomato.

So, where's the food I'm supposed to cook for the big breakfast? Not in this refrigerator. That would mean a grocery bill, which she won't reimburse me for, and it would mean going to the grocery tonight for this breakfast to happen tomorrow morning.

She frowned and shook her head. *No, Beverly. Not happening.*

Marcie considered what she knew about the woman she was house sitting for.

Very little. Less than she usually knew about a client.

What's she really like?

Marcie had only spoken to Beverly once on the phone, after Zeke had set up the meeting.

The woman was certainly a control freak, but one of the nice things about house-sitting was the fact that the home-owner was away and not in your face, forcing you to have to deal with their micromanaging.

With a phone call, you could distance yourself a little, put them on speakerphone, and move across the room to fold your laundry, or do whatever else needed doing.

Best way to deal with anyone going off on a rant was to get distance.

She took out a bottle of water, uncapped it, and took a swallow.

Now to meet Ginger.

The little dog had been barking since Marcie had let herself into the house with the key that had been under the mat on the front deck.

Ordinarily, she would have put meeting the dog first on her list.

She'd been told to go find the note first, to read it before letting Ginger out, and to put the key back under the mat, where the cleaning lady could find it.

Beverly was going to have the house "thoroughly cleaned," but she didn't say when, or leave any information about the cleaning lady.

Marcie always did her best to follow her client's directions, so she put the key back under the mat, but she didn't feel good about it. It didn't seem like the safest idea. But, without knowing how to get ahold of the cleaning lady to make other arrangements, she didn't have much choice.

Usually, she would put the client's house key on her key ring right away and never take it off until the job was done. Then she'd return it exactly where she got it. She'd never lost a key or been locked out. Not once.

Ginger was still barking and sounded wound up. Probably because a stranger was in her house. The little dog had only been left alone for an hour, as Marcie had made sure to arrive as close to the time Beverly and her boyfriend Zeke had left as possible.

If her flight hadn't been delayed by an hour, she'd have been there right after they'd left, as planned.

I'll let Ginger out, and I'll check to make sure all the windows and doors are locked from the outside.

Later, she would check from the inside.

These habits were for her safety and had developed from moving into strange houses in towns she'd never been in before.

You couldn't always count on everything being secure. Homeowners were often careless, particularly when their minds were on going out of town.

It was Marcie's job to keep an eye on the house, contents and any pets, and it was one she took seriously. There'd never been a theft on her watch, and she intended to keep it that way.

So far, the front door to the living room and the sliding glass doors in the kitchen were the only doors she'd gone in or out of, but that didn't mean the others were locked, or that the windows were locked. People often forgot.

Here in ski country, did it ever get warm enough to open the windows?

None of the windows looked like they even opened. This was her first time staying on a mountain in ski country in a chalet-style house.

Maybe here, on top of the mountain, it didn't get warm enough to open windows.

She'd entered through the front door, and pocketed the key, then moved through the living room and then down the three steps off to the right, ending up in the kitchen, where the instructions were on the table.

Ginger barked and barked.

Marcie felt bad about not going to the little dog right away, but she was following the homeowner's instructions.

It was important to read the instructions first. Sometimes there were directions as to the care of the pet.

It's best to learn what you can about the pet, before meeting them. That way you'd hopefully learn anything important and could ease any distress the pet might feel at meeting a stranger who had entered their house.

This time she'd been given little information about the dog.

Beverly was more interested in the elf than her own dog.

The note had barely mentioned Ginger. There were no instructions for her care. Marcie sighed and tried not to be judgmental.

Checking the sliding glass doors, she paused to look out at the snow-covered view. A blanket of white covered everything.

The view sure is pretty.

Leaving the note on the table, she headed for her first meeting with Ginger, leaving the kitchen, moving past a small bathroom, and into the next room at the back of the house.

Ginger barked again.

"Coming, Ginger," she called. "I hear you, and I've heard all about you."

Actually, she hadn't. Hadn't been told where the dog crate was, what Ginger's favorite toys or food were, or any tips to make dog-sitting any easier for either of them.

The only thing she'd been told over the phone was, "You're a dog-sitter. You know what to do."

Well, yes, I do know what to do, but still. Beverly gave more instructions on that weird elf than she did on her own dog. And that elf just sits there. It doesn't need anything.

Her dog, Ginger, on the other hand, is a living creature, with a personality, feelings, and needs. You'd think being away for an entire month, her owner would care more about her dog than a silly old elf and an online contest. Money prize or not.

How does Ginger do with strangers? Well, I'll soon find out.

Inside the crate, a brown-and-white King Charles Spaniel barked and wagged her tail furiously. She had the sweetest face, and her coat was shiny and untangled.

She's been groomed. At least she looks cared for, not neglected. It's time to let her out.

The closer Marcie got; the more excited Ginger became.

Marcie laughed as she reached into her coat pocket, to touch the doggie treats she had brought with her. "You lost your warning bark, Ginger. That's a 'pet me please' bark, if I ever heard one."

Ginger's tail wagged even more furiously.

The minute Marcie unlatched the door, Ginger rushed out and stood barking happily, wagging her tail.

"Well, you are just adorable," Marcie said. She loved seeing happy dogs and knowing that she made them happy.

Ginger responded with kisses and tail wags, which wagged her whole body, making Marcie laugh.

Dog-sitting could be so much fun.

"It's nice to meet you too, girl," Marcie said. "Do you need to go out?"

The little dog responded with more wiggles and tail and body wags in her excitement. The soft, cuddly dog had plenty of energy and plenty of welcome kisses for her new dog-sitter.

Holding off on a treat for now, Marcie reached for a nearby leash and clipped it to Ginger's collar.

Once Ginger was on her leash, they moved past the bathroom and into the kitchen, toward the sliding glass doors, which led to the front deck.

Ginger stopped in front of the kitchen table, refusing to go farther, and began barking furiously at the elf, as ferocious as a King Charles Spaniel could be, her tail no longer wagging. Instead, she went from barking to growling at the elf.

Marcie wasn't thrilled with the elf either, but she wondered what it was about the elf that had made the dog so upset.

The previously sweet-faced, happy little dog now appeared as if she wanted to tear that elf apart. The sudden switch in behavior was a bit unnerving, and Marcie wasn't sure how to handle the situation.

Acknowledgments

It takes a team to put a book out into the world.

This story would not have been completed on time and nearly as well without the help of former LEO Charlene Leber Lancaster. Thank you for beta reading, and for the multiple edits of this story. Charlene went above and beyond.

Thank you to Destry W. Stevens from Greybull, Wyoming for letting me borrow the name Destry and for his excellent care when I was in the Billings Clinic for 18 days in the summer of 2023. The rest of Destry in this story is entirely fiction as far as words, actions, and events. However both Destrys share a level of caring and encouragement which are present in the very best of nurses. From the moment I heard the name Destry, I knew I needed to write this book. And coming out of ICU with a blood clot still in my brain, it was encouraging to know that my creative imagination was fully intact, even if I couldn't start writing the book yet.

My cover artist, Sheri L. McGathy created this amazing cover.

Thank you to the Bartlett Citizens Police Academy for the ten weeks of training, which gave me a base of knowledge to write from and to Bobby Buls, my gun instructor and advisor.

Thank you to Charles "Tazz" Welshans, the first bull rider I've met, for answering my early questions about rodeo. And to all the rodeo cowboys I've watched and learned from since. Thank you to my husband for answering questions about horses and rodeo, and to Doenne Brown for explaining rodeo events.

Thank you to SEAL veteran and author Bill Hellman for feedback, advice and encouragement on SEALs and Delta Force operatives.

My continual thanks to Melissa Ammons, my virtual assistant, who helps in many ways.

My husband, Mike, is much more than the bus driver of our 43 foot rig. I've needed his help with many things since the 2023 stroke, especially since I still can't drive which means he has to drive me everywhere. Forty four years married, and we are still having adventures, and hopefully will have many more.

To each reader who picked up this book: thank you for taking a chance on my story. Your time is valuable and I'm honored you chose to read one of my books. I hope it keeps you turning the pages, and that you enjoy the story.

To all my returning readers: Thank you for your support through the years, especially these last two. It feels good to be back with a new story. I love being able to share my stories with you and hearing that you enjoyed them.

To every reviewer who has taken the time to read and review my books, I appreciate you! Reviews are essential to a book's success and I love hearing what you think of my stories. I read every single review.

Most of all, thank you God, for helping me to survive that stroke in the summer of 2023, and helping me to regain the ability to read a line of text and the ability to write again. I feels wonderful to have finished a story with all new pages and I'm ready to write another!

Thank you to my UNC Chapel Hill neural PT team

who have worked with me for over a year to build new neural pathways in my brain and get my life back. And to all the medical people from UNC Chapel Hill who've helped me improve my health.

Thank you to every single person who prayed for me and who continues to pray for my healing.

I love you all.

"Every day we are alive is a beautiful day," and I am thankful every single day for that.

- Debra Parmley

About the Author

Author Debra Parmley believes "Every day we are alive is a beautiful day," and she likes to give her readers and her story people a story that ends happily.

An Air Force veteran's wife, Debra writes suspense/thriller, military romantic suspense, contemporary military romance, historical romance, urban fantasy romance, fairy tale romance, holiday romance, poetry, and memoir.

Debra married her high school sweetheart, whom she asked out after a five-dollar bet. After living in five states with her husband and their two sons, and then living 23 years just outside Memphis, TN, she and her husband sold everything in 2020 and now live and travel the U.S. in their 43-foot motorhome full-time.

Debra is an adventurous writer who has climbed lighthouses because she is afraid of heights. She worked as an independent travel agent and has set foot in more than 13 countries. She has walked the plank of a pirate ship off the coast of Grand Cayman, and gone swimming with dolphins in Moorea's waters, in French Polynesia. She once escorted a bus full of people through Scotland.

Disabled in the summer of 2023, after a stroke, she continues to enjoy living and traveling in their motorhome.

You can read about her travels on her Beautiful Day Traveler blog https://beautifuldaytraveler.wordpress.com/ and also

Follow Debra's Beautiful Day YouTube Channel: youtube.com/channel/UC27hTWse4gLJxTETQw6i7xw/ for travel videos as well as videos of Debra reading first chapters from her books

Visit www.debraparmley.com

As Debra Bishop, she writes fairy tales for all ages, fantasy, and children's books coming in 2025. Visit https://debrabishop.com/

Also by Debra Parmley

MILITARY ROMANTIC SUSPENSE:

Single Title:

Montana Delta Rodeo Cowboy: Bodyguard Protector

To Catch an Elf : Pennsylvania Fighter Pilot

Aboard the Wishing Star

Green Brotherhood SEAL Team XII series:

Finding Bryce, book one

Real Movie Hero, book two

Saving the Bellydancer, book three

Green Brotherhood Trilogy #1

Bobbins Sisters Trilogy:

Check Out – book one

Check In – book two

Check Mate – book three - 2025

Brotherhood Protectors series:

Montana Marine - book one

Defensive Instructor - book two

Marine Protector - book three

Marine Protectors - box set

Blind Trust - book four

A Triple C Ranch Christmas Wedding

Montana Delta Rescue - book six

Montana SEAL Protector - book seven

* * *

URBAN FANTASY ROMANCE:

Vague Directions: Into the Woods

* * *

WESTERN HISTORICAL ROMANCE:

Gone to Texas: A Desperate Journey

Dangerous Ties

Deadly Adversaries

Desperate, Dangerous, Deadly: A Western Collection Isabella, Bride of Ohio: American Mail Order Bride

* * *

1920's ROMANCE:

Butterflies Fly Free series:

Trapping the Butterfly – book one

Dancing Butterfly – book two

Exotic Butterfly – book three

* * *

HOLIDAY ROMANCE:

Jenna's Christmas Wish

The Twelve Stitches of Christmas

* * *

DYSTOPIAN ROMANCE:

The Hunger Roads Trilogy:

Another Change of Scenery

Down a Back Road

Into the Convergence Zone

* * *

NONFICTION:

Anywhere But Here: Our First Year Full Time RV Living on the Road – 2025

* * *

POETRY ANTHOLOGIES:

Twilight Dips

Everything Begins in the Belly

* * *

Out of Print:

Protecting Pippa

Split Screen Scream

Protecting Zarifah

Vague Directions – short story

A Desperate Journey

Isabella, Bride of Ohio

Tales of Deadwood - anthology

We Know the Truth, Do You? Area 51 – anthology (going to the moon/time capsule)

Wounded Heroes - anthology

Hansel & Gretel: Down the Rabbit Hole – anthology

More Monsters from Memphis – anthology

* * *

WRITING AS DEBRA BISHOP:

Fairytales:

The Sweetest Day - Hansel and Gretel fairytale
Children's: coming in 2025.

* * *